BEN THE DRAGONBORN

A SIX WORLDS STORY

DIANNE ASTLE

Six Worlds Publishing

www.benthedragonborn.com

Dianne Astle/Six Worlds publishing
www.benthedragonborn.com

Publisher's Note: This is a work of fiction. Names, characters, places, and incidents are a product of the author's imagination. Locales and public names are sometimes used for atmospheric purposes. Any resemblance to actual people, living or dead, or to businesses, companies, events, institutions, or locales is completely coincidental.

Book Layout © 2014 BookDesignTemplates.com

Ben the Dragonborn/ Dianne Astle. – 2nd ed.
ISBN 978-0-9921626-1-0

The Six Worlds Series:
Ben the Dragonborn 2013, 2015
Ben and the Watcher of Zargon 2015

.

This book is dedicated to my children
and to Allison who lent her name to a character in this book.

CONTENTS

CHAPTER ONE

SINK OR SWIM

Create It was 9:30 in the morning. Ben Taylor sat by a swimming pool, his feet dangling in the water. Ben's head rested on his clenched fists. His brilliant green eyes were closed. His unruly dark brown hair had not been brushed. Anyone who looked closely could see that Ben was trembling.

At any moment the Physical Education teacher would call Ben's name. Phil Tanner expected Ben to jump into the swimming pool, do the front crawl to the other side, and return with a backstroke. Ben was not sure he could even stay afloat, let alone do two different strokes across the width of the pool.

The request that he swim across the pool was not unreasonable. Ben had been taking swim lessons for three months with his grade nine class. Not that Ben attended very many classes. He usually found some excuse. For a couple of weeks, he had a sniffle that turned into a raging cold just in time for the swim lesson. For a couple of weeks, he sported a thick bandage on his big toe. It covered a scratch, but only Ben and his roommate Denzel Carter knew the truth. Another week he managed to see a dentist when he should have been in the pool. Then the excuse was a sprained ankle. It was a legitimate excuse—he had suffered a mild sprain; however, Ben's limp was much worse when it was time for swim class. Ben's excuse this week was that he could not find his bathing suit. This excuse had worked once before, but this time Phil Tanner was prepared. Tanner handed Ben a suit left behind by a previous student: a student three times Ben's size.

"Allison Sims," Phil Tanner called. The girl sitting next to Ben slid into the pool. Ben's mouth went dry. He clenched his hands even tighter, but they still shook. Taylor followed Sims on Phil Tanner's list of students.

Allison made it look so easy. She swam effortlessly across the pool and back.

"Well done," Phil Tanner said as Allison gracefully slid out of the water to sit beside Ben once again. She rubbed water out of her blue eyes and looked at Ben with concern. Ben's eyes remained closed. Allison took one of her copper colored braids in each hand, leaned towards Ben and squeezed. Ben jerked away as cold water hit his shoulder.

"Wake up, Ben," Allison said. "You're next."

Ben said nothing. He was normally tongue tied around Allison, but always worked hard to come up with a witty response. This time he did not even try. His thoughts were consumed with what he would do when his name was called. He was desperate to find an excuse, any excuse to stay out of the water.

Phil Tanner spoke the words Ben was dreading. Ben hesitated, desperately searching for an excuse, but his mind was blank.

"Come on, Benjamin," barked the teacher. "Into the water! We don't have all day."

Ben jumped and immediately knew it was a mistake. He sank like a stone. He came up spitting water, his arms and legs thrashing. Ben's frantic movement took him slowly forward in the required direction. For a moment Ben had some small hope that he might actually get to the other side. Then the bathing suit slipped down over his bum. Ben grabbed for the suit, but it was impossible to keep his head above water with only one hand free to dog paddle. So Ben did what any sensible person would do. He let go. The swimsuit slid further down and Ben quickly learned it is impossible to kick your legs with a swimsuit wrapped around your knees. Staying afloat demanded that he kick so Ben decided to retrieve the suit after all. Mustering his courage, he bent into the water and reached towards his knees.

It is a simple fact that when one part of the body goes down, another part rises up. None of the eight girls and ten boys missed the fact that Ben mooned them. They pointed, hooted, giggled, hollered, and laughed out loud.

"Girls to the change room," Phil Tanner ordered. All the girls left, except for Allison.

Ben didn't hear the laughter. He had more important matters to deal with. He was swallowing pool water and the swimsuit was not cooperating. It was hanging around his knees. Spots gathered in front of Ben's eyes. His arms and legs were beginning to feel heavy. Everything was going black as he finally kicked off the bathing suit.

Phil Tanner was not watching Ben. He was puzzled as to why Ben was such a poor swimmer. He was counting the absent marks beside Ben's name in the record book. He muttered, "Taylor, you have some explaining to do," and slammed the book shut. He needed to speak to the substitute teachers who taught for him when he was away.

"Mr. Tanner! Mr. Tanner!" An urgent voice broke the Physical Education teacher's concentration. Phil Tanner transferred his attention to Allison Sims, who was standing before him.

"I said girls to the change room. That includes you."

"But Mr. Tanner, Ben needs help," Allison persisted. Phil Tanner looked up to see Ben's borrowed swimsuit floating on the water, but no sign of Ben.

Phil Tanner pushed his record book into Allison's wet hands, and dove into the pool. In a few quick strokes the teacher reached the swimsuit, jackknifed, and with eyes wide open swam underwater. The teacher found Ben and dragged him to the surface. When Allison saw that Phil Tanner had Ben in tow she did as she was told and left, after giving the record book to one of the boys.

Phil Tanner dragged Ben out of the pool and threw a towel over his naked body. Then the teacher began to press on Ben's chest. One…and a two…and a three. Water flowed out of Ben's mouth, but he was still not breathing. Phil Tanner pinched Ben's nose. He took a deep breath and bent over to give Ben mouth to mouth.

At that moment Ben took a deep shuddering breath. Phil Tanner let go of Ben's nose, but remained hunched over the boy. That was a mistake. Ben brought up the considerable breakfast he had eaten earlier. It spewed in all directions. Pieces of orange and bacon hung in Phil Tanner's hair.

There was shocked silence at first, then suppressed laughter from the boys in Ben's class.

"Everyone to the change room," Phil Tanner roared after wiping oranges and bacon off his face. When everyone was gone the teacher shouted at Ben. "Tomorrow, before breakfast and every morning after that, I want you here with a *swimsuit that fits*," Phil Tanner thundered.

"No…I…don't wa…" Ben started, unsure of just what to say.

"Failure is not an option for the son of Andrew Taylor," the teacher continued, without listening to Ben. "You will have another test next Monday and every Monday after that until you pass."

By the time Ben arrived at the boys' change room, everyone else was nearly dressed. There was suppressed laughter from everyone but his roommate Denzel. Denzel held a towel towards Ben in his dark hand. His brown eyes were full of concern. "You okay?" he asked.

Ben shrugged as he took the towel; he was afraid words might bring tears.

"Do you want me to wait for you?" Denzel asked. Ben shook his head no.

Ben took a long shower. The water was cool, but Ben did not turn off the tap until the talk and laughter died down and the door banged shut for the last time. When he finally turned off the tap, a clock hanging on the wall told him math class had already started. He rammed one wet leg and then the other into his blue jeans and struggled into his shirt. He picked up his socks, but realizing they would be too hard to put on wet feet shoved them into his gym bag. He threw the gym bag over his shoulder, stuffed his bare feet into his runners and sprinted out the door.

"Ben! Wait!" called a voice, "Are you okay?" Allison was waiting for him outside the change room door. Concern was clearly written on her freckled face.

Ben shrugged. "You'll be late for math."

"You too, but I'm sure you could write the test later. Almost dying is a good excuse."

"Uhgg. I forgot the test."

"Like I said, you could take the test later."

"I might, but what about you?" Ben replied, as they left the Physical Education building and ran towards the castle.

Ben and Allison were students at Fairhaven Private School. Fairhaven was a school for students from grade nine to twelve, where it was as important to learn to hang glide and rock climb as it was to learn algebra. Most students had parents and grandparents who attended Fairhaven before them. But there were a few like Allison, who received a special invitation to come. There were only fifty-eight students at Fairhaven. They came from many different countries of origin. Money or the lack thereof was not a barrier as no one paid tuition.

The school was located on its own private island in the Pacific Northwest not far from the small community of Gold River, British Columbia, Canada. Through natural means it could only be reached by boat or float plane. However, many students reached the school by means that were far from natural. There were portals in various parts of the world that brought students to Fairhaven the moment one stepped through them.

As well as the Physical Education building, there were residences for students and teachers, a stable, barns, and chicken coops. There were horses in the stable as riding was part of the curriculum. Most of the island was forested, but the area close to the school had gardens, hayfields and a pasture, as well as sports fields. The school farm grew most of the food eaten in the dining hall. The surrounding ocean provided fresh fish.

The largest building on the island was a small castle made of large gray stones. A pathway led from a small secluded bay to the wide front steps of the ancient building. The stone steps led to two large oak doors. In the basement were the community kitchen, dining hall, and common rooms. On the main floor were classrooms and offices. The second floor had guest quarters and an extensive library. The third floor held a large meeting hall, as well as the office space and residence of Mariah Templeton, the principal of Fairhaven. On the fourth floor there was a small deep pool and a hexagonal shaped room with six walls and six doors. No one was allowed on the third and fourth floors without an invitation.

Ben and Allison stopped and stared when they reached the castle. To Ben's dismay, the large swimsuit hung out the window. Words in large print said, "Lose something, Ben?"

"Oh no. Now everyone will know," Ben muttered.

"Everyone was going to know anyway. This is a small school," Allison responded before sprinting up the stairs.

Ben steeled himself for laughter when he walked through the classroom door, but there was no laughter. Yoko Suzuki was away. In her place was William Smith, a substitute teacher with a permanent scowl on his scarred face.

"No point in asking to postpone," Ben whispered. "Smith would insist a corpse write the test."

"And the corpse would if it knew what was good for it," Allison whispered back.

William Smith glared at them with his one good eye. His other eye was covered by a black patch. Where his left hand should have been there was a hook. William Smith used his right hand to beckon Ben and Allison forward. He growled, "You're late. Five percent will be deducted from your marks."

"But…" Allison began.

William Smith, cut her off, "I am being lenient, since I understand Taylor came close to death this morning." He passed them a copy of the test with his hook.

Ben took his seat behind Denzel, who flashed Ben a quick smile, his teeth white against his dark skin.

As the students finished, they silently filed out of the classroom, until only Ben and Allison were left.

"Time's up," William Smith said in his gravelly voice, just as Ben finished the second to last question. Ben and Allison laid their tests on the desk in front of Mr. Smith.

"So I understand you haven't learned to swim yet, Taylor," William Smith growled.

"I'm not planning to learn," Ben stated flatly.

"That's a problem."

"Doesn't matter, I'll just stay out of the water."

"It matters! You get serious and listen to me. Anyone can learn to swim and that includes you."

Ben started to turn away, but the substitute teacher grabbed Ben's sleeve with his hook. "Hear me, Ben Taylor, and hear me good. I don't want to hear about you missing your swimming lessons. You are not going to disappoint your father. He is my friend and one of the best students this school has produced."

Ben jerked his sleeve out of the hook's grasp and sprinted for the door. Denzel was waiting for him on the other side.

"You O.K?" Denzel asked.

"Yeah," Ben said. "I hope Suzuki is back soon. Smith is just plain scary."

"Too true! But then there are a lot of scary teachers at this school. And Smith isn't the only one with battle scars. It's creepy."

"I wonder where Suzuki went?" Ben asked.

"Who know? She's away a lot," Denzel responded. "So is Tanner and some of the other teachers. I'd like to know where they go and why we have so many substitutes."

The two friends walked to their next class. Throughout the day, Ben had more than one teacher and several students offer him advice on what to do in the water.

That night Ben had the same dream that he had almost every night since coming to Fairhaven. It was dark. Two moons hung in the sky. His mother had disappeared. Ben was flying through the air, suspended by the claws of a giant scaly bird. Over and over he cried, "Momma, Momma." Tears ran down his cheeks. The creature holding him gave a piercing cry and released its hold. Ben fell through the air into deep dark water. The cold stunned him. The blackness terrified him. He tried to call his Momma, but no sound came. There was only water. He couldn't breathe.

Like always, Ben woke with his heart pounding and his fists clenched. His breath came in shuddering gasps. Denzel stood by his bed; hand on Ben's shoulder, shaking him awake. "For Pete's sake Ben, see a shrink. Find out what these nightmares mean. I'm tired of waking up every night," Denzel said in a tired, irritated, but concerned voice.

The clock said it was quarter past two. Ben lay awake, afraid to fall asleep. He did not want to dream again, but by three he was sound asleep.

The next day Ben had the required private swim lesson. It was a disaster. Mr. Tanner had to jump into the pool and fish him out once more.

CHAPTER TWO

HIDE AND SEEK

After supper the next day Ben and Denzel went to the library. They watched students go in and out of a part of the library forbidden to them.

"Look," said Denzel, "Allison is allowed to go in there. Why aren't we allowed? She's grade nine and so are we."

"Don't ask me," Ben said, just as a bell rang. He listened for a moment. It was a special bell the grade nine's had been told to ignore.

"It's not for us." Ben said to Denzel.

"I know, but look," Denzel pointed, as students and teachers filed out of the forbidden section of the library.

The librarian, Olivia Stewart, wheeled her chair out from behind a desk. "The library is now closed. Take whatever books you need. Bring them back tomorrow."

Ben put his books away. He stood and was starting towards the door until Denzel jerked his arm with such force that Ben found himself sitting back down on the chair.

"What the…" he began. Denzel put a finger to his own lips and dropped under the table. Ben followed him muttering, "This is a bad idea, a very bad idea." Nevertheless he crawled underneath the table with Denzel.

At the end of the table, Denzel crawled between two bookshelves, then stood and sprinted to the far end of the library. Ben followed.

Denzel dropped to the ground and pushed himself underneath a study desk. Ben stood staring down at him as Denzel gestured in silence for Ben to crawl underneath another desk. Ben stood undecided. It was not too late to leave, but he had to make a quick decision. Someone was coming. The steps were getting closer and closer. Someone was checking to make sure no one was left inside the library. Finally Ben made up his mind and dropped to the ground. He pushed himself underneath a second study desk. The footsteps stopped between the desks where Ben and Denzel lay hidden. The footsteps belonged to a trusted grade twelve student, appointed to monitor the halls and make sure the rules were not being broken. Ben held his breath until the feet turned and walked away. After a moment they heard a door close and the library was silent.

"This is a bad idea," Ben repeated as he climbed out from under the desk. "A very bad idea."

"Yeah, probably, but at least it's not boring," Denzel replied. Being bored seemed to be the one thing in life that Denzel was frightened of, perhaps the only thing, from what Ben could tell.

"Nobody gets a chance to be bored around you," Ben muttered. "A little boredom would be welcome now and then."

"Let's go," Denzel said. Ben did not need to ask where.

Denzel pushed open the door with its "ENTRY FORBIDDEN WITHOUT SPECIAL PERMISSION" sign and Ben followed him in. They both knew it was a mistake as soon as they stepped through the door. There was a loud clang as the door bolted behind them and the lights went out. Since there were no windows in the forbidden section of the library it was very dark. Ben whirled around and felt for the door handle. It confirmed his suspicion that they were locked in.

"O.K. What are we going to do now?" Ben asked in a squeaky voice.

"Look around," said Denzel, as he dug into his pocket and produced a small flashlight. He swung the flashlight first this way and then that. The light rested briefly on a sign: Zargon. In the middle of the library were several small tables with books open on them. Denzel walked to the nearest table and ran his flashlight over the books. He picked up one whose cover read, "The Six Worlds: Their Similarities and Differences." He turned to the table of contents. Listed in alphabetical order were six worlds: Earth, Farne, Lushaka, Mellish, Toregan and Zargon. Denzel turned his flashlight away from the book to the "Zargon" sign. He shone the flashlight around the room and found the other five signs. He turned back to the book and opened it to the section on Zargon.

"The most important difference between Zargon and other worlds," the book began, "is that dinosaurs and dragons still live on Zargon, while they have disappeared from the other worlds where they once existed."

That was as far into the book as Denzel, with Ben looking over his shoulder, was able to read. They heard the library door open and close. Denzel turned off his flashlight and put it away seconds before Phil Tanner opened the door of the darkened room. Phil Tanner found them standing in the dark and was unaware of the flashlight in Denzel's pocket.

"Out! Now!" Phil Tanner thundered. He hustled the boys out. "I will see you tomorrow. And I would count on a very long detention if I were you."

Ben groaned. Detention meant working in the kitchen—peeling potatoes, loading the dishwasher and washing pots and pans.

The boys were escorted to the stairs and ushered out of the building. They wisely left the castle and went back to their dorm room. The next day the two friends were called into Mr. Tanner's office and given two months of detention starting that very day. They reported to the kitchen and worked for an hour before and after supper. As they peeled and scrubbed, they talked quietly of what it might all mean.

"There is something going on in this school," Denzel said, "and I intend to find out what it is."

"Did you notice that Allison came out of the forbidden section of the library when the bell rang?" Ben said.

"No, I didn't, but I'm not surprised you did. I think you have a crush on that girl."

"So what do you think's going on? Why are there books about imaginary worlds in the forbidden library?" Ben asked, trying to change the subject.

"I think it's some kind of role-playing game. Maybe everyone gets assigned an imaginary world and becomes a character in that world."

"So the bell rings when it is time to play?"

"Yeah, I guess."

"I'd love to be in on the game."

"Me too. I wonder how you get an invitation?"

"Maybe Allison will tell us," Ben said, blushing.

"If you can actually talk to her, she might," Denzel said.

Over the next few days they tried to talk to the students who were able to go into the special part of the library but were rebuffed. Allison went out of her way to avoid them after they asked several times why Allison could go into the library and they couldn't and why the bell rang for her and not for them.

Three days later, Ben and Denzel finished their detention in the kitchen and were heading up the stairs to the library when the special bell rang again. They watched as students and teachers filed past them and went up the stairs to the meeting hall.

"Come on," Denzel said. "Let's see if Allison will talk to us."

"She won't talk," Ben said. "We've already tried several times."

"Allison, wait!" Denzel shouted.

Allison moved in front of some grade twelve students and continued up the stairs to the third floor. Denzel tried to follow, but two older boys blocked their way. "You're not allowed on the third floor without an invitation."

"How do you get an invitation?" Denzel asked.

"You'll know when you do," the older student said.

Denzel and Ben stood aside and watched teachers and students climb the stairs into the great hall. There were no other grade nines besides Allison included in the gathering.

"Come on," Denzel said, "We're going to find out what's going on up there."

"And how are we going to do that?" Ben asked.

"We're going to look through a window," Denzel stated.

"What window?"

"I'll show you."

Denzel led the way down the hallway. They passed Olivia Stewart, as she waited in her wheelchair for an ancient elevator to take her to the third floor. Denzel led Ben to the math classroom. He opened a window and started to climb through.

"What are you doing?" Ben exclaimed.

"Putting the rock climbing we've been learning into practice. Why do you think they teach us these things if we're not supposed to use them? You comin'?"

"No! Definitely not! I don't want to break my neck."

"I've always wanted to do this," Denzel said as he stood on the ledge and searched for a handhold.

"Denzel! Don't do it!" Ben spoke loudly. "Fall and you'll be dead!"

"Shhhh. I'm not going to fall," Denzel replied in a loud whisper as he began to climb.

Ben waited, wondering how he would explain his presence in the math classroom if a teacher came in, although that seemed unlikely as they were all on the third floor.

Ben stuck his head out the window and watched Denzel move slowly up the rock wall, carefully searching for and finding handholds. When Denzel reached the third floor window, he pulled himself up over the ledge to look in. Ben watched Denzel gasp and his foot slip. Ben was afraid that his friend was going to fall, but Denzel grabbed the window ledge with his right hand. Denzel dangled for a moment before finding a handhold to begin his climb down. Ben helped a shaken Denzel back in through the window.

"Well?" Ben asked when Denzel was silent for an uncharacteristically long time.

"She knew. Miss Templeton knew I was there. She leaned forward and looked right at me, our eyes met. I tried to duck and that's when I lost my hold."

"What were they doing?"

"Just sitting around; but someone, I don't know who, was dressed up as a mermaid. Great costume. Greenish skin, blond spiked hair with green tips. The eyes had no whites. The tail was amazing. It was worth the climb just to get a glimpse of that vision of beauty."

"Weird!" Ben said. "We might be right. It is a role-playing game. I wonder what world is supposed to have mermaids. I wonder if they assign you a character or you choose it for yourself."

"I don't care, I just want in. We need to find out what it takes to join," Denzel stated.

The two boys hung around the castle. When the meeting ended, they managed to catch Allison just before she entered the girls' dormitory.

"Allison," Denzel said. "What were you all doing up there?"

Allison stared at him for a moment, then shook her head, and ran up the stairs. Denzel started to follow, but Ben grabbed his arm.

"You want to have detention till you graduate? Going into the girls' dorm is one way to make that happen."

CHAPTER THREE

TIME FOR TEA

In the morning, Ben ate early and headed for the swimming pool for his extra lesson with Phil Tanner. The lessons were still not going well. This one was no exception. Ben did not feel comfortable in the pool even when his feet were able to touch bottom. Phil Tanner was waiting for Ben when he left the dressing room.

"I've called Miss Templeton, Ben. She wants to see you today after your last class. I told her there is little hope that you will learn to swim. I'm really sorry about that."

"It's not your fault. I have always hated the water. I don't care if I ever learn to swim," Ben said.

"I care and your dad cares. He is going to be very disappointed," Phil Tanner said. He paused a moment and then continued, "Your dad and I were roommates. He has been my best friend for over twenty years. I don't know how to tell him that I couldn't teach his son to swim."

Later in the day, Ben walked slowly towards the castle and up the stairs to the reception area on the third floor. Mrs. Topp, the school secretary, sat at a desk near the stairs. On one side of her was the door to the great hall and on the other side was the door into Mariah Templeton's office and residence. Ben had been on the third floor twice. The first time was when his father brought him to the school.

They had climbed the stairs together and Mariah Templeton had come out of her office to welcome him. A week into the school term there was a gathering for students and teachers in the great hall to which everyone was invited. Mariah Templeton spoke to the students. She spoke of the students as chosen ones who would bring light to dark worlds. Ben laughed at her words, until his father had glared at him. Later when he had tried to tell his father how strange Mariah Templeton was his father had been unwilling to listen.

Ben's father had come back to the school a month later. Andrew Taylor told Ben that he was going away on business, but expected to be back within six to eight weeks. Eight months had passed and his father had not yet returned. The end of the school year was coming and Ben wondered if his father would return in time to take him home.

Andrew Taylor had often gone away on business when Ben was a boy. His grandmother used to take care of him until his father returned, but now his grandmother was dead. Ben wasn't sure where he would end up this summer, but more importantly he was worried about what had happened to his father.

"Miss Templeton wants to see me," Ben announced to Mrs. Topp.

Mrs. Topp pushed a button and spoke into an intercom, "Ben Taylor to see you, Miss Templeton."

"Good! Send him right in," Mariah Templeton replied.

Ben had never been in Mariah Templeton's office before. The first thing he noticed was that the high walls were covered in pictures. Some of the pictures had an otherworldly look to them, featuring creatures that only exist in the pages of storybooks. Others seemed to be moving. It seemed that when he looked a second time at a picture the scene had changed. They were the kind of pictures the head of a role-playing society might be expected to have in her office. However, Mariah Templeton did not look like a woman who spent a lot of time playing games.

Mariah Templeton was an elderly woman with gray hair pulled back in a tight bun. Wire rimmed glasses perched on her nose. She wore a dress that had not been in style for over fifty years. Around her neck was a very large pendant. The pendant was gold and covered in Celtic knots that had no beginning or end. The knots swirled in and around six rubies. Such an ornate pendant looked out of place on the plain-looking, elderly woman.

Ben entered the office and stood before the desk where Miss Templeton sat. Across from the principal were two chairs. One of the chairs was a normal, stuffed leather chair with wooden arms. The other was an elaborate golden chair, with a high back. Every inch of the metal chair was covered in etchings and Celtic knots with no beginning or end. In six places there were groupings of precious stones. The chair looked like it belonged in a throne room rather than the office of a school principal. Ben put his gym bag on the floor beside the leather chair and waited for Principal Templeton to invite him to sit.

"Tea, Mr. Taylor?" Mariah Templeton asked in an accent that Ben could not place.

"Um, okay. I mean, yes please."

"Would you like cream or sugar?"

"Yes, please…both," Ben replied.

Mariah Templeton poured tea for him, adding cream and sugar. She pushed the cup across the desk towards the elaborate golden chair. "Please be seated," she said. Ben reached for the cup and started to move it towards the leather chair, but Mariah Templeton stopped him. "Not that one. You must sit on my special chair."

Ben moved to the metal chair and sat down. It was cold against his back. He felt very uncomfortable in this strange chair. It was too tall and his legs dangled. Mariah Templeton poured herself some tea and then sat staring at Ben.

"You must have inherited that hair from your father," Miss Templeton said. Ben ran his hand over his unruly hair in a futile effort to put it back into place. "But those eyes are extraordinary. I've never seen another Earthling with eyes like that."

Ben choked on his tea. Miss Templeton made it sound like she'd met green-eyed aliens.

"Those eyes remind me of someone." Miss Templeton glanced quickly to a picture hanging on her wall. "Interesting," she said, with a perplexed look on her face.

"I don't recall ever meeting your mother, Ben, which I find strange," Miss Templeton continued. "I make a point of getting to know the families of all my students. Do you look like your mother?"

"Dad says I have her eyes."

Mariah Templeton frowned and glanced once more at the picture on the wall.

"Your father and I met for the first time when he was about your age. He was an outstanding student and has been a friend of the school ever since."

"Have you heard from my father?" Ben asked.

"No, I haven't…yet," Mariah Templeton frowned and her lips tightened, a worried look appearing momentarily.

"He said he'd be back in one month, two at the most, and now it's been almost eight months."

"Things sometimes take longer than expected, but I'm sure he's fine. Your father has handled many challenging situations over the years. He knows what he's doing and he will be back as soon as possible. Now please tell me about your mother."

"She died when I was young."

"That might explain why I don't remember her. But tell me what you remember."

"I remember very little that makes sense," Ben replied, thinking of his recent dreams.

"What has your father told you?"

"My father doesn't talk about my mother much, but I know he misses her a lot."

"What was your mother's name?"

"Zinder."

At the name Zinder, Mariah Templeton gave a small gasp and sat up straighter. She stared at the picture she had glanced at earlier. Ben followed her eyes to the picture and saw a dragon looking into a mirror. In the mirror was a woman with red hair and brilliant green eyes.

Ben stared at the picture as he said, "That's a strange name isn't it? Dad says she was smart and beautiful, and very brave, and that the only thing I seem to have inherited from her is my eyes."

"How did your mother die?" Mariah Templeton asked, still looking at the picture.

"Uhhh…" Ben hesitated; he could not remember his father actually saying anything about his mother's death. It was his grandmother who had told him she had died. "I think—a car accident," Ben finally said, with no real idea as to why he said it.

The principal took a long slow drink of tea. "So am I to understand that your father raised you by himself?"

"Yes, but my grandmother lived with us until she died two years ago."

"Ah yes, your grandmother was also an outstanding student. She was the first of your family to come to Fairhaven, and now you might be the last. From what I understand you're afraid of water."

"Lots of people are," Ben said defiantly. "It's not a big deal."

"It is here. Our students are asked to take journeys that begin and end with water. The journeys are the whole reason that we have a school here at Fairhaven."

"Guess I won't be going anywhere then," Ben said decisively.

Mariah Templeton ignored him. "Our students undergo a test," she said. "It is usually given at the end of grade nine or beginning of grade ten, but some take it earlier and others later, depending on when they appear to be ready. There are generally two or three, sometimes more, from every class who fail. I am going to give you that test now. If you pass, you WILL learn to swim. If you fail, we will discuss your future at this school when your father returns."

Principal Templeton's words disturbed Ben. He liked Fairhaven. He did not want to leave, but all he said was, "W...w...w..what kind of test?"

"A simple one. But let's finish our tea first."

Mariah Templeton asked Ben questions as they finished their tea. Ben had a hard time with the questions as all he could think of was the possibility that he might not be able to return to Fairhaven for grade ten.

"How do you like Fairhaven?"

"It's great! I want to stay here until I finish grade twelve."

"What's your favorite subject?"

"I love the horseback riding lessons. You don't get that at most schools."

"How do you and Denzel get along?"

"He's great. Denzel's my best friend."

"Does the food agree with you?"

"Yeah. I like the food."

"Do you have any idea where your bad dreams come from?"

The last question surprised Ben. He wondered how the principal knew about his dreams. Denzel was the only one who knew and Ben was sure that his friend wouldn't tell anyone.

"No," was Ben's only reply to the last question.

When they finished their tea Mariah Templeton walked around her desk and came to stand beside Ben. She took Ben's hand and laid her pendant on his open palm. As Ben watched in amazement, the front of the pendant began to move. The front opened up as flowers do to the sun. Inside were three circles: One for the days of the month, another for the months of the year, and the third with the years in a century. An arrow in each of the circles pointed to today's day, month, and year. Ben did not know what this test was meant to prove, but nothing happened. The arrows did not move.

Mariah Templeton took the pendant out of Ben's hand and put it back over her neck and returned to her chair.

"Just so. Benjamin, it appears that there is no need for you to learn to swim. You are free to leave and join Denzel in peeling potatoes. Hopefully the two of you will learn to avoid detentions in the future. I will talk to your father when he comes back about where you will go to school next year." Miss Templeton could not prevent her voice from conveying some of the disappointment she felt.

Ben put his hands on the arms of the chair to push himself out of it. Light began to shine underneath his hands. He tried to remove them, but they seemed to have become stuck to the chair. Soon the whole chair was glowing. Light shone out of every etched line. If he could have Ben would have leapt from the chair, but the light wrapped itself around him and held him in place.

"It appears I was too hasty," Mariah Templeton said in surprise. "With great pleasure Benjamin Taylor, I tell you this. You have been chosen by the Guardian as were your father and grandmother before you. The dials on my pendant did not move because your first journey is to take place this very moment."

Ben sat in stunned silence, unable to move or talk. Light streamed out of every etching on the chair and swirled above him and around him. The light seemed to penetrate right through Ben's body. It flowed through his mouth, his eyes and his ears, and appeared to come back out through the center of his chest.

Mariah Templeton stood with her hands resting lightly on Ben's head saying words that he did not understand. Ben's hands felt odd, as did his feet. His shoes suddenly felt too small. Miss Templeton picked up one of his hands and turned it over. Running along each finger and up into the palm were suction cups that reminded Ben of an octopus.

"Ah," said Mariah Templeton, "you will be able to climb what needs to be climbed and hold fast when you need to."

As Ben looked down at his body it disappeared from sight.

"And you will be invisible when there is a need. Now what will be your third gift?" Mariah Templeton wondered aloud.

Principal Templeton waited and Ben waited with her. But nothing else happened. The light drew back and disappeared into the etchings. There was silence, then Mariah Templeton exclaimed, "I don't understand. There should be a third gift. There are always three gifts given."

Ben stammered, "W...wh...what happened?"

"Good news, Ben. You are to follow in your father's footsteps. You have been chosen by the Guardian of the Six Worlds to go to a world that is not your own. You should have been given three gifts, but never mind the third gift will likely manifest itself later."

Ben remained silent.

Mariah Templeton began to chant. "Benjamin Taylor, chosen of the Guardian, you are called to serve justice and peace. Where you go, the Guardian goes. The Guardian will be your companion as you defend and protect the weak, restore peace, and bring hope to the peoples of the six worlds. May the light of the Guardian dwell in you always, and may you be a source of light in those places where shadows gather."

"I don't understand!" Ben said.

"You will," Mariah Templeton stated.

Ben wondered if Miss Templeton had put something in his tea to make him hallucinate. He was anxious to leave her office.

"Come Benjamin, it is time to go," Mariah Templeton commanded.

Ben stood up with relief. He picked up his bag and headed towards the door he had come through.

"Not that way, Ben. This is the door you need to go through today," Mariah Templeton commanded. She walked to the door behind her desk and opened it. Behind the door was a flight of steps. Ben realized that he was about to find out what was on the mysterious fourth floor of the castle.

Ben followed Miss Templeton through the door and up a flight of steps. At the top of the steps were three doors. Miss Templeton opened the one in the middle and they entered a room with six walls. Each wall had a door in the middle of it, including the one they had come through.

Mariah Templeton took her pendent and laid it on Ben's open hand once again. Ben watched as the pendant opened up. This time he did not see three circles. Instead of three separate circles pointing to the day, month and year, there was a compass. The needle pointed north towards the door Ben had just come through. As Ben and Mariah Templeton watched the hand on the compass began to move. It turned towards the west and stopped.

"Not that door. I do not want to send you to that world with just two gifts," the principal muttered. "In fact, I do not want to send anyone else to that world for the time being. Not until I find out what happened to the Zargon Watcher and to…" Miss Templeton stopped, glanced at Ben and did not finish her sentence.

The compass started to move again. It slowed at each of the doors and finally came to rest pointing to a door on the northeast wall.

"Oh dear," breathed Mariah Templeton. "This is a problem. This is not a good choice for someone afraid of water. And rarely is anyone asked to go without the gift of being able to breathe under water. Maybe I shouldn't send you at all. And yet, it is clear that the Guardian intends for you to go to Lushaka this very day. I could wait, but lives might be lost. But if I send you…" Again, Mariah Templeton did not finish her sentence. "This is difficult," the principal continued, speaking to herself. Then she fell silent, as she contemplated the choice before her.

Ben broke the silence. "I should get back to the kitchen and help Denzel." The principal ignored him.

Ben looked at Mariah Templeton with growing agitation as she stood beside him with her eyes closed trying to decide what to do. Finally, she spoke, "My job as a Watcher is to prepare and send through the portal those that the Guardian chooses. You have been chosen. Therefore, I must send you. The Guardian of the Six Worlds chose you because you have the best chance of success. Even if I do not understand how this can be, it must be so. You must go. Maybe your third gift will come when you step through the portal. I hope it is the gift of breathing under water."

Ben had come to the conclusion that the principal of his school was a nutcase; however, when she commanded that he follow her to the door on the northeast side of the room, Ben did as he was told. Mariah Templeton opened the door to reveal a stone wall. Ben was relieved. There was no water in sight. He was not going to be expected to step out into thin air.

The brick wall did not faze the principal at all and she proceeded to ask the following questions. "Benjamin Taylor, in the name of the Guardian, will you stand against evil? Will you go and serve the cause of justice and peace? Will you defend the weak against those who would crush them?" Mariah Templeton looked expectantly at Ben.

"Ahhh," Ben began, wondering what to say. However, Mariah Templeton took his "ahhh" as an affirmative.

"I, Mariah Templeton, Watcher of Earth invite you, Benjamin Taylor, chosen of the Guardian to go through the portal to bring the light of hope, the promise of peace, and the joy of freedom to the people to whom you are now sent. Go forth in the name of the Guardian to bring honor to earth and to your ancestors by what you do."

"Once your work on Lushaka is complete," Miss Templeton continued, "you are to return to Earth until the Guardian of the Six Worlds has need of you again."

Ben just stood there and stared at Miss Templeton in silence.

"The best way to go through the portal the first few times is with your eyes closed; that way you will not be confused by what you see."

Ben closed his eyes.

"Now," instructed Mariah Templeton, "step forward and continue stepping forward until you are through the portal."

Mariah Templeton put her hand firmly on Ben's back and gave him a gentle push. Ben stepped cautiously forward. He took one step and then another and another. He was puzzled and wondered why he had not run into the wall. Ben took a large step, anxious to hit the wall so that he could show Miss Templeton that people did not walk through solid walls. He desperately wanted to leave. Detention had never looked so good. Ben took a bigger step, sure that this time he would hit the wall, but he did not.

Ben opened his eyes and saw blue sky. He looked down and saw water below him. A look of sheer amazement quickly passed across Ben's face to be replaced by sheer terror as he fell through the air. Ben's nightmare was becoming a reality. He was falling from the sky into water.

CHAPTER FOUR

RESCUED, I THINK

The gym bag saved Ben's life. It had a rubber lining and was well made. With the zipper closed it held air—at least temporarily.

Ben floated on top of it. Every once in a while he lost his balance and was dumped into the water, but he had his arm through the strap of the gym bag and never lost his hold on it.

"This is just a dream…this is just a dream… just a dream," Ben repeated over and over again. Logic told Ben that this whole horrible day was a new variation on the nightmares he'd been having. Yet the water was wet, the sun warm, and everything felt very real.

Whenever Ben lost his balance he got a taste of the water, which was sweet rather than the salty water that surrounded Fairhaven.

The gym bag was slowly losing air. Ben wondered what would happen when all the air was gone. Would he wake up, or would this be the day of his death, the day his nightmare became reality.

The water was quite warm, but Ben's teeth chattered anyway. Ben was not only afraid of sinking below the waves, but he was afraid of what might live in this much water. As he thought about what might lie beneath he pulled up his feet, but became unstable. He had no choice but to kick gently as he scanned the horizon, looking anxiously for land.

As if fear had conjured it up, a fin broke the surface about ten feet away. Ben pulled his feet as close to his body as he could without losing his balance. He tried to stop his teeth from chattering, but they chattered even louder.

When the water began to swell about two feet away, Ben let go of the gym bag. It went one way and he went the other. With nothing to hold onto Ben sank below the gentle waves. He held his breath, closed his eyes and kicked his legs frantically, which caused him to bob back up to the surface. He waited in dread for whatever terrible thing was about to happen. When an attack did not come, Ben opened his eyes.

"Hello," a musical voice trilled.

Shock caused Ben to stop kicking and he sank below the waves. He came up sputtering with his eyes open. There was no doubt. This was all a dream. There in front of him, holding his gym bag and looking at it with great, big, curious dark eyes, was a girl. A girl like no other Ben had ever seen. She had dark brownish-black eyes with no white and short blond hair with green tips that stood up in spikes all over her scalp. It was a girl like the one Denzel had claimed to see. This girl was staring at Ben with a quizzical look on her face.

"Wh...wh...who...who..." Ben began, but anything else he intended to say was lost as he sank beneath the waves once more. He forgot to hold his breath and came up spitting water. When he opened his eyes the girl was wiping spit off her face with one hand while holding onto the gym bag with the other. Ben grabbed the bag from the girl and held onto it as if his life depended on it. He floated on the water as he stared at the girl in astonishment.

"Have you seen anyone else around here? Someone older than you? Someone with muscles? Someone special? Someone who doesn't spit on people they don't know? Someone who knows how to talk?" As she hammered Ben with questions the girl swam circles around him. The final question was, "Someone who just drops out of the sky?"

Ben stared at the girl.

"Well?" she asked, "Have you?"

"No, I... this is ridiculous. You're not real. None of this is real. There is no water. There is no girl."

The girl reached out and pinched Ben's ear.

"Owww!" Ben howled.

"Does that feel real to you?"

"What are you doing out here?" Ben asked. "I don't see land nearby. How did you get here? Do you have a boat?"

The girl ignored Ben's questions. "No, I guess there is no one else. You must be the one. They must have run out of real heroes to send a boy like you."

The last statement irritated Ben for the girl was not any older than he was. Ben had never met anyone so rude. Ben decided right then and there that he did not like this girl, real or imaginary. He was beginning to suspect she was real. He doubted he could imagine someone this obnoxious.

Ben tried once more to ask the questions the girl had ignored: Where is land? Do you have a boat? To Ben they were the only questions that mattered at the moment. The girl continued to ignore Ben's questions.

"Come with me," she said and dove head first into the water.

"Wait...don't go," Ben began. Then he simply stared, speechless. As the girl's head disappeared a large tail fin rose gracefully out of the water. Ben was stunned. He stared at the place where the girl had disappeared. He watched anxiously for the couple of minutes that it took for her to return.

"Y...y...you are a m...mermaid!" Ben stammered.

"Of course. What else would I be?" the girl said. Then she stopped and stared at him for a minute before speaking again. "Who are you and what are you doing here?"

"I...I...I... don't know where here is. All I know is that I walked through a door and ended up here." Ben paused and then said slowly, "I think I'm the one you're looking for."

"I find that hard to believe, but I was sent here to find a Chosen of the Guardian and you are the only person I have found, so I guess I'll take you to the Watcher and Lea Waterborn will decide whether you are the one."

"I w…w…w…want to go with you. The problem is I can't swim. I also can't breathe under water," Ben said, remembering what Miss Templeton said about the third gift often being the ability to breathe under water.

The girl stared at him with her mouth hanging open. Then she gave a high-pitched whistle. In less than a minute two more fins broke the surface; fins that were attached to what Ben would identify as orca on earth, except they had longer jaws that contained some vicious looking teeth.

The mermaid flipped her tail a couple of times and joined the two orcas a few feet away from Ben. She spoke to the orcas and all three of them turned and looked at Ben as he hung helplessly on top of the gym bag. It appeared to Ben that the orcas laughed, if orcas can laugh, at whatever the girl said about him. The mermaid then said something else and the two orcas shook their heads. The mermaid became agitated and Ben caught snatches of what she said, "mistake…wrong…Watcher will decide." Then one of the orcas gave a barely perceptible nod and the three of them swam towards Ben.

"This is Akca and Osch, and my name is Charla," the girl said. She did not ask Ben what his name was, but talked rapidly on. "Akca has agreed to let you ride on his back. He will carry you to the Watcher. I hope you know this is an honor rarely granted."

Ben looked at the orca. He was not sure he wanted to be so honored. Akca looked distinctly unhappy. In fact, it seemed to Ben that the orca would be happier having him as the main course for dinner.

"Isn't there any other…?" Ben began.

"No, there isn't. You can stay here or you can come with us. It's up to you," responded Charla curtly.

Akca swam alongside Ben. It took all the courage Ben possessed to let go of his gym bag and grab hold of Akca's dorsal fin. Once he had a firm grip Ben swung his right leg over Akca's back.

Osch grabbed the handle on Ben's gym bag and with a toss of his head threw it into the air. It came to rest just behind his head. Osch led the way. Akca followed with a speed that took Ben by surprise. It was like being dragged behind a motorboat. Ben lost his grip and was soon floundering in the water. Charla and the orcas laughed. Akca swam alongside Ben once more. Ben grabbed his dorsal fin and pulled himself back onto the orca's back. Ben was determined not to let go this time. But once again he lost his hold and ended up sputtering in the water. Charla did not laugh this time. Neither did the orcas. This time Akca gave a few high-pitched squeals as he came back to pick Ben up. As they started off Ben wished for the suction cups he had imagined in Miss Templeton's office. He no sooner thought of them when he felt a change occur on his hands and feet. After that, he had no trouble holding on.

Charla swam alongside Akca and Ben. She touched Ben's arm and pointed up to the right. Ben followed her finger with his eyes and saw a speck to the right high above them.

"When I tell you to, take a deep breath, and hold on tight," Charla directed. "We will go under water."

Ben shook his head vigorously. "No, I can't."

"You must," Charla responded. "Now!"

Ben took a deep breath just before Akca dove under the waves. They hid under the large leaves of a water plant and watched the surface where the only thing that remained was Ben's gym bag. Ben almost forgot to hold his breath when he saw a giant bird swoop down and scoop it up. The bird was far bigger than any Ben had seen or heard tell of. It had a razor sharp beak. Cold black eyes stared out from a bald red head. Its feathers were black with red accents on the tips of its wings and tail. Something about that bird made Ben glad that he had not been floating on top of his gym bag.

Spots were gathering in front of Ben's eyes when they returned to the surface. The bird was flying back the way it had come with Ben's gym bag suspended from its talons. Ben laid his head on Akca's back. His breath came in great shuddering gasps. When his breathing had just about returned to normal Charla said, "Are you okay? Can we continue on now?"

Ben nodded his head in affirmation. As they resumed their trip, Ben scanned the sky, alert to the possibility that danger might come from above rather than from the sea below.

As they traveled, the water became shallow. The bottom was visible in places. Multi-colored fish swam in and among plants that grew towards the sun. Giant, solid-looking water lilies lay on the surface of the water. The occasional tree grew up from the bottom of the sea. They had just passed a grove of such trees when Ben saw a welcome sight; a small island. It was the first land Ben had seen since his arrival.

Akca brought Ben alongside some steps cut into the rock. Ben was so anxious to get his feet on dry ground that he tried to jump off while he was still attached to Akca by suction cups. He remained glued to Akca, who squealed unhappily as he was turned over on his side by Ben's weight. Ben wished fervently that the suction cups would disappear and they did. There were small round marks on Akca's back where Ben's hands had been.

Ben climbed the steps, grateful to be back on solid ground. He waited for directions. Charla swam towards the steps with two flicks of her tail. She placed her hands on the first step above the water line. Then she curled her tail up under her body and pushed up with her hands. Rising up out of the water was not the tail of a mermaid, but two very human legs. The only thing that remained of Charla's tail was a very short skirt made of fish scales. It matched the tight-fitting top she wore.

Ben stood there with his mouth hanging open. "How can you...?" Ben began and then decided it was no stranger than anything else that had happened.

Charla climbed the steps and moved past Ben towards a cave. "Are you coming?" she said.

Ben followed until they were just about to enter the mouth of the cave. He froze when a large snake emerged from the cave. Its head rose higher and higher until it towered over Charla and Ben. Ben saw himself and Charla mirrored in the snake's lidless eyes as it stared down at them. Its tail was hidden inside the recesses of the cave. The snake's head reared back and sped forward. Ben took hold of Charla's waist and threw her sideways. He fell on top of Charla. The ground sizzled close to where Ben and Charla had been standing. Ben rolled off Charla and scrambled up. Smoke rose from where the venom had hit the ground.

Ben reached down and lifted Charla to her feet. The snake's head followed their every movement and another volley of acid hit the ground just in front of them. Charla seemed frozen by fear. Ben struggled to drag the mermaid back to the water with him. Ben wondered if she had even seen the snake.

"Snake, big snake, acid!" Ben yelled.

Charla still hung back. Another gob of acid hit off to the right. A fern growing where the acid hit burned. Still Charla was not moving. Ben continued dragging her toward the water. But he let go of the girl's hand when he realized that Charla was laughing. He looked back to where the snake had been, but it had disappeared.

Ben scanned the area but saw no sign of the snake.

"What was that?" he asked.

"It's an illusion," Charla said. "The Watcher created it to keep out any human that might wander in looking for a dry spot to make camp. Pretty effective, huh?"

"Very!"

The ground still smoldered. Smoke still hung in the air. But on the ground where the acid hit nothing was changed. The fern Ben saw burn was untouched.

Charla walked back towards the cave. It took all the courage Ben possessed to follow her. He closed his eyes and kept walking when the snake reappeared. He opened his eyes in time to see the snake's head hurtling towards them. Ben jumped aside. He couldn't help himself. Charla snickered and kept walking. The snake's head went right through her and broke apart. Ben hurried after Charla and walked through the dissolving illusion into the mouth of the cave. The body of the snake still lay on the floor. As Ben walked his feet broke the illusion apart.

The rock wall at the back of the cave was covered in what looked like drawings done by a primitive people. Charla reached out and traced one of the many patterns. Her fingers lightly touched the rock as they traced the outline of a roughly drawn fish. She went around the outside of the fish three times, changing direction each time. When Charla completed the third circuit a low rumbling sound began and grew stronger. The rock wall in front of them split in two and slid back into the walls on either side. They walked through the opening and the doors closed behind them. They had no light, but the cave was not completely dark. On the walls, on the floor, on the ceiling there were pinpricks of light that came from small rocks. It was enough so that Ben could see his feet on the path. He could also see Charla's smirking face.

CHAPTER FIVE

TO BE OR NOT TO BE

As they walked into the heart of the island, the light-bearing rocks became more numerous and it became easier to see. They walked until they came to a place where the tunnel opened up into a large bright cavern. On one side of the cavern was a pool. On the other side, the cavern floor was flat rock. In the pool there were a dozen mer and the two orcas. Outside of the pool, there were mer in their human form involved in the kind of martial arts training that Ben was getting at Fairhaven. Circular steps went around a flat-topped pillar in the center of the cavern. From the flat top of the pillar, rope ladders suspended from the ceiling led in four directions to a ledge that circled the upper walls of the cavern. Behind the ledge were cave openings, some of which were fitted with doors.

Charla led Ben towards the pool. Akca and Osch were talking to a mer woman who sat with her tail in the water. The mer woman's green-tinged blond hair was done in dreadlocks and pulled back and tied in a ponytail at the back of her head.

"How did they get here?" Ben asked, pointing to the orcas.

"There is an underwater passageway, which is how we usually bring in visitors."

Charla and Ben stopped and stood waiting while the mer woman continued to talk with the orcas. One of the woman's hands rested lightly on each of their heads, gently stroking them. The woman looked inquiringly at Ben. Her eyes, like Charla's, were large and dark with no white at all. The woman stared at Ben for a moment, then turned and spoke to the orcas. They disappeared. The mer woman brought her tail out of the water and laid it on the ground in front of her. Ben watched the tail transform into two legs, beginning with the feet and moving up. When the transformation was complete, she stood. The older woman was dressed in a similar manner to Charla. She wore a simple fish scale top and short skirt. Around the mer woman's neck hung a pendant identical to the one that Miss Templeton had.

For a moment there was an uncomfortable silence. Then the woman said, "Charla please introduce our guest."

Charla flushed with embarrassment, "Uh, I forgot to ask his name, but he's not the one."

The mer woman stared at Charla for a moment then finally said, "How can you be so sure of that?"

"He can't breathe in water. He can't even swim."

"That is odd; however, it would be odder for a human Lushakan not to be able to swim than it would be for someone from off-world."

The woman turned her attention to Ben. "I am Lea Waterborn, the Watcher of Lushaka."

"Lushaka?"

"The name of our world," Lea Waterborn replied, clearly surprised that he did not know where he was. "Normally a chosen would know what world they were going to before they went. They would prepare for their journey by spending time in the library that is part of the school on each world."

"If he was a Chosen, he should know what world the Guardian was sending him to, and if he is Lushakan he should know the name of his own world. Maybe all we have here is a Jellybrain!" Charla exclaimed.

Lea Waterborn gave Charla a stern look before turning back to Ben and asking him a question. "What is your name and where are you from?

"My name is Benjamin Taylor." Ben paused and then added, "and I'm from Earth."

Lea Waterborn's eyes widened slightly.

"Charla," said Lea Waterborn, "please ask housekeeping to find Benjamin some dry clothes and ask the kitchen to send food to my office."

At the mention of dry clothes and food, Ben realized how very hungry he was. "Dry clothes and food would be very welcome," Ben said gratefully. Whether what he was experiencing was real or a dream he still felt a need to eat.

"And Charla," the Watcher continued, "please find Brina and ask him to come to my office."

Charla's face fell, but she said nothing. The Watcher saw her disappointment and said, "All right, you can join us as well, since Ben arrived during your watch."

Charla's face lit up and she hurried off to order food and find Brina.

"Please come with me Benjamin Taylor," Lea Waterborn said,

"Ben, people usually call me Ben."

"Ben it is."

Ben fell into step beside Lea Waterborn as they walked to the stairs and up to the second level. The students in the practice field and the pool had stopped their exercises to watch them. On the stone and rope walkways, people stopped where they were and stared. Male and female mer alike all had green-tinged blond hair and dark eyes. They all wore similar fish scale garments.

The first thing Ben noticed when he entered Lea Waterborn's office was that it had a chair much like the one that Ben had sat on in Mariah Templeton's office. It sat by itself at one end of the room. At the other end sat six chairs in a semi-circle. Each chair had a footstool in front of it. Between every two chairs there was a small table. Lea Waterborn led Ben to the circle of chairs. "Please sit," she instructed.

"I'll wait until I have dry clothes on," Ben said.

The Watcher sat down in one of the chairs and placed her feet on the footstool. As Ben watched, her legs turned back into the tail of a mer woman.

"What is the name of your Watcher?" Lea Waterborn asked.

"Miss Mariah Templeton." Ben guessed that she knew the answer, but wanted to know if he did.

"And the name of your school?"

"Fairhaven."

"Clearly you are from Earth and I assume you are the right one."

"I'm not sure about that," Ben said. "I think someone has made a big mistake. If this is not a dream, I shouldn't be here. I was sent to Miss Templeton to talk about my fear of water, and somehow ended up in a world that has more water than I ever imagined in my worst nightmares. Someone has made a huge mistake. I'd say—" Whatever else Ben was going to say was cut off by a knock at the door.

A male student entered and brought dry clothes, which he handed to Ben. The boy was introduced as Brina. Ben took the dry clothes and changed behind a screen that Lea Waterborn directed him to. Afterwards he sat in the chair the Watcher offered him earlier.

Charla arrived with a tray of food and cups of juice. The only things Ben recognized were eggs. Charla identified the unknown food as pickled sea slugs, sea cucumbers, as well as a seaweed and snail salad. Ben ate some eggs and a little of the cucumber.

After they had eaten, Charla looked back and forth between the Watcher and Ben, her fingers drumming on the arm of her chair. Finally, Charla was unable to contain herself. "Is he or is he not the one?"

"He is the one...but this day has been a challenging one for Ben because he knew nothing of the Guardian, the six worlds or the portals before today."

Charla seemed stunned, "But...but..."

And while Ben tended to agree with Charla, he felt somehow vindicated by the Watcher's words.

The Watcher turned her attention to Ben. "You seem to have some doubts as to whether this world is real. Please act as if it is in spite of your doubts. Your life might depend on doing that."

This sounded like good advice to Ben.

"You have the gift of holding fast," Lea Waterborn continued. "I saw the marks on Akca's back. He was not happy, but I assured him that they would disappear. What other gifts do you have?"

Ben remembered the strange experience in Miss Templeton's office. "I think I have the gift of invisibility."

"That gift can be very useful," Lea Waterborn said, "although you must remember that if a creature depends largely on its sense of smell it will be able to find you anyway. What is your third gift?"

"There is no third gift," said Ben. "Not that I know of anyway."

"Are you sure?" asked the Watcher clearly puzzled.

"Miss Templeton said that a third gift might come later. She hoped it would be the ability to breathe under water."

"And that did not happen?"

"No. Are there always three gifts? Ben asked.

"Yes and no," said the Watcher. "There are actually four gifts. One is always given. The ability to understand the language of the people to whom you are sent is always given. There are certain groups who receive only two other gifts because they already have a third gift that came to them at birth. For example, the Mer chosen by the Guardian always have the gift of transforming their tail fin into legs. When we travel from our world we are given two additional gifts besides the ability to walk and understand the speech of others. The two additional gifts are ours to use when we are away from our world, but once we return to Lushaka the gifts return to the giver."

"Who is?"

"The Guardian of the Six Worlds, of course," exclaimed Charla. "Don't you know anything?"

The Watcher gave Charla a sharp look before continuing on, "On a world called Zargon there are a people who can transform into dragons. As far as I know, only mer and the dragonborn have an inborn ability to transform. Not every mer on our world can transform into human form. Not every human on Zargon can assume a dragon form. On Lushaka there is a great distrust of those who can transform and so we find it better to hide our ability from other mer and Lushakan humans."

Ben thought of the picture in Miss Templeton's office. The picture of a dragon looking into a mirror with the image of a beautiful woman reflected back. It seemed quite unbelievable that such a being could exist. But here he was having a conversation with two mer females and a mer man on a world that was not his own. Who knew what was possible on another of the six worlds? Unless, of course, he had fallen asleep and was dreaming and none of this was real.

"People from earth normally are given three gifts besides the gift of understanding other tongues," the Watcher continued. "I do not understand why you would only have two. It is a mystery to ponder. But now it is time to speak of the purpose for your being sent here. Not far from here there is a problem. Mer and humans are coming close to war. It all began when one of the giant birds, which we call Tregs, took the crown from the head of the King of the Silverfish clan. The Mer King has decreed that humans cannot fish or gather food from the sea until the crown is returned. The King believes the sea belongs to him and humans should get the crown back for him out of gratitude for being allowed to harvest food from the sea. He will not listen to reason. The humans have tried. Some of our mer elders have tried. The humans have sent their strongest and best to retrieve the crown. So far, none have returned. The humans grow desperate. Almost all their food comes from the sea. If the situation continues, they will have no choice but to go to war."

"I don't understand what I'm expected to do!" Ben said with conviction. "If people who know this world and its dangers can't get the crown back, what am I supposed to do? Even with these two gifts?"

"I don't know, but it will be revealed to you when the time is right. The Guardian chose you because you have the best possible chance of success with the gifts you have been given."

"Does the Guardian ever make mistakes?" Ben asked.

"The Guardian does not make a mistake in who is chosen." When Lea Waterborn said this, Charla snorted, which let everyone know that she thought a mistake had been made this time.

"As I said," Lea Waterborn continued, "the Guardian does not make a mistake in who is chosen, but those who are chosen go into ever changing situations and there are no guarantees of success."

"Why don't you send someone from here? I saw lots of…"

"Yeah! Why not? Charla interrupted. "We don't need this jellyfish. We can get that crown back on our own."

Lea Waterborn ignored Charla. "The Guardian prefers that the Chosen not interfere with the affairs of our own world. There are dangers in doing so. Power is so easily misused. It is easy to convince yourself that what benefits you and yours is good for all the peoples of your world. The Guardian gives gifts that we are to use to help other worlds, who will in turn help us. Lushakans have risked their lives many times on earth. They do it with gratitude for the help that has come to us in our time of trouble from the other five worlds. Most Chosen would know of these things, but you do not because it came as a surprise to Mariah Templeton that you should be chosen without time to prepare."

"As to whether you decide to help or not," Lea Waterborn continued, "that choice is yours to make. The Guardian never forces us to do what we do not want to do. If you choose not to go, the Guardian of the Six Worlds will find someone else to send. It will take time, and the person sent will have less chance of success than you do.

Your refusal may mean the death of Lushakans as we wait for another to come, but if you wish, I will send you through the portal back to earth. The magic given to your Watcher will ensure that you forget you have ever traveled to another world. But know this Benjamin Taylor, you will never be chosen again. The loss is yours as well as ours. You will miss living the life you have been chosen for. Your life will forever feel the loss, but you will never know just what it is you have lost. If you do accept this challenge, there is good reason to believe that you will be successful because you are the one the Guardian has chosen, but know that there are no guarantees. Some have fought the good fight and not won the day. Some battles are lost, but the fight continues on. I suggest you sleep on it, and tell me in the morning for it grows late."

The Watcher turned to Brina. "Brina, please take Ben to our guest quarters." Lea Waterborn's tone became stern as she spoke to the mer girl. "Charla, please stay, as I would speak with you alone."

Brina transformed and stood. Ben followed Brina out of the office. They walked across the cavern on one of the rope walkways. Brina took Ben on a tour of Fairwaters before taking him to the sleeping quarters. When they reached the guest room, Brina pointed out a cord Ben could pull if he needed anything during the night.

The guest quarters consisted of a small room with a table, two chairs, and two single beds. Ben undressed, and climbed into one of the beds. He pulled a light blanket over himself.

Ben was tired but he could not fall asleep. He kept thinking about the decision he would need to make in the morning. He had a strong feeling that someone had made a huge mistake in choosing him to come to this world. How could someone who was afraid of water be the best choice on five worlds? In the wee hours of the morning Ben fell asleep, but when he did the nightmare that had plagued him for many months visited him. This time it was more vivid than ever before and contained details that had been missing in his previous nightmares. As he fell from the sky Ben looked up and saw a moon overhead. Flying in front of the moon was a large scaly creature. It gave the piercing cry that had been part of Ben's dreams for several months.

Ben woke up and lay awake thinking about what his answer would be in the morning. How could he possibly stay in a world where there was so much water? How could he stay in such a world, surrounded by the one thing that he was most terrified of? If this was a normal world, where there was land under his feet he would stay and do what he could to help, but how could he stay here? After much thought, Ben decided that he was going to return to earth in the morning. It was the only choice he could make with his fear of water.

"This person they call the Guardian, must have made a mistake. Denzel should have been sent instead of me," Ben thought.

With the decision to return to earth made, Ben fell asleep.

CHAPTER SIX

A MISTAKE

Ben woke to a knock. He was still trying to recall where he was when the door opened and in barged Brina. Ben looked at Brina with bleary eyes still heavy with sleep.

"Rise and shine. And if you can't shine, it is still time to rise. You don't want to miss breakfast. The Watcher will want to see you right after."

Brina pulled off a curtain that covered a bright patch of light-emitting rocks. Then he grabbed the blanket and ripped it off the bed. He picked up the clothes that lay scattered on the floor and threw them at Ben. Pants, top, and socks flew through the air. It wasn't until a shoe came down with a thud on his head that Ben sat up. "Hey, stop that."

"So sorry," said Brina with a chuckle.

Ben was truly awake now. He sat up in bed and pulled on his clothes.

Brina led him along the ledge overlooking the pool and practice field and through an archway into a large dining hall. There were a number of mer sitting at tables. Most had transformed from legs to tails, which they rested on a large central beam that was part of the underside of each table.

"Why do mer transform when they sit?"

"It is natural for us. It takes energy for us to maintain legs."

Brina led Ben to a table near the kitchen to pick up his food. One look at the food told Ben that breakfast was a repeat of what was served the night before. He took some eggs and a little sea cucumber. Brina led Ben to the nearest table and introduced him to a mermaid named Shirl who was about Ben's age. Brina left after asking Shirl to take Ben to Lea Waterborn's office after breakfast.

"How do you like it here at Fairwaters? Is it much like your school?" Shirl asked.

"I haven't been here long, but there are similarities."

"How many students are at your school?" Shirl asked.

"There are fifty-eight," Ben responded. "How many students are here at Fairwaters?"

"There are only twenty-one actual students. Any mer who can transform are brought here, but not everyone is a chosen."

As Ben looked around the room he saw a small group of young mer sitting at a table with legs rather than a tail. He pointed them out to Shirl, who said, "Those students must spend the day without transforming. This happens several times during our training. The first time is short, but the time is increased until we can spend a week without returning to our natural form. It is hard for us, but necessary, if we are to be chosen to go to other worlds. Those who cannot last a week will never be chosen. Their training comes to an end. To fail is a great disappointment, not just for the student, but often for their family, as well."

Ben was quiet for a moment as he thought of his own father. Where was his father? Did his father go through a portal? Those times when his father left home on business was he on one of the other five worlds? Had his father been a chosen all along? Ben felt sure that he had. Miss Templeton said something about Ben following in his father's footsteps. It struck Ben that his father would be disappointed if his son refused to try to help the people of this world. If his mother and grandmother were still alive, they too might be disappointed.

"How many students from your school go through the portal in a year?" Shirl asked.

Ben responded, "I don't know. I knew nothing about Watchers or the Guardian until yesterday."

"That is a surprise," Shirl said. "I'm going to Earth in a month and I've spent a lot of time studying everything about your world: its countries, people, and creatures. What I am really curious about is a Venus Fly Trap. Have you ever seen one?"

Shirl asked all kinds of questions about Ben's school, his family and his world. Ben answered her questions to the best of his ability. Shirl would have asked more but a bell rang. "Come on, Ben. We must go. Class is starting and I need to take you to Lea Waterborn first."

Shirl led Ben to the Watcher's office. "I hope to meet you again when I come to your world. It will be an honor to be able to serve your world as you are now serving mine," Shirl said before she left Ben.

Ben remained silent. He did not tell Shirl that he planned to return to Earth. Ben turned sadly away and knocked on the office door. He waited until he heard the Watcher invite him to come in.

When Ben entered Lea Waterborn's office, he was surprised to see a human boy a couple of years older than himself there. His first thought was that his replacement had already been sent. Ben was surprised when the Watcher did not introduce them. "Have you made your decision?" she asked Ben.

Ben was surprised to hear himself say, "Yes, I'm going to stay." It seemed like there was nothing else he could say. As he spoke these words, he knew it was the right decision, the only decision he could make. He could go back, and if what Lea Waterborn said was true, he would forget about ever being on another world. Perhaps his father would not be too disappointed; however, he knew he would never be free of his own sense of disappointment in himself. He might not remember, but Ben feared that he would always have the sense that his life was not what it could have been.

"Good," said the Watcher. "I anticipated your response. Therefore I have made arrangements. Akca and Osch will go with you. As will Brina."

Lea Waterborn then spoke to the boy, "Brina make sure you stay to the west of the caves of Chard…"

"Brina!" Ben exclaimed.

"Yes, it's me."

"I would have never guessed," Ben said.

"Good!" Brina exclaimed.

Ben looked carefully at the boy beside him. Brina was wearing contact lenses. The eyes looked human, not mer. He was wearing baggy shorts and a woven shirt that pulled over his head. The spiky hair had been shaved close to his scalp. On earth, he could easily pass as an ordinary boy.

"As I was saying," Lea Waterborn continued, "stay to the west of the Chard Caves. There is a human community beyond the caves that you will need to avoid with a war about to begin. Hopefully you will not meet any mer, which is another good reason to stay away from the caves. There may be mer gathering there for a battle with the humans."

"Where are we going?" Ben asked.

"The information I have tells me the source of the problem is likely on Spencer Island. About eight months ago there was a change on that island. I noted that the natural order of things on the island was disrupted. I sensed the change through the bond I have with my world as its Watcher. Eight months ago my connection to the island became fuzzy. It was like it ceased to exist for me."

When Lea Waterborn saw the puzzled look on Ben's face she added, "Watchers have a connection to the world they serve. Through our bond with the Guardian, we know things about our world without being told. We usually know when and where there is a problem. We can sense where evil is building up and where people cry out in pain. We know when the natural world is in distress. I should have some sense of how things are on Spencer Island, but I don't. What I do know is that the tregs from that island have started acting strangely. They pick up things they had never shown any interest in before. Things like the Mer King's crown."

Ben looked from one worried face to the other and said, "I'm glad Brina is coming with me, but I thought you said Brina could not be one of the chosen on his own world?"

"That's true," responded the Watcher, "he is simply going with you as a guide. The only gift Brina takes with him is the ability to transform and walk on human legs."

"By the time I get back to Fairwaters, I won't think of it as a gift," Brina said.

Turning once more to Brina, Lea Waterborn said, "Brina, unless you have no choice, stay in your human form until you are back at Fairwaters. I do not need to tell you that it would put both your lives in danger if you were seen transforming. I wish I had a boat to send you on. It would be safer than traveling on our ocean dwelling friends. There will be awkward questions if you are seen riding our friends. However, the last storm destroyed the only boat we had. It was so rarely used that I have not been in a hurry to replace it."

"I don't understand," Ben said. "Don't the chosen use boats?"

"No, almost everyone comes with the ability to breathe under water. However, this experience has taught me that it is important to have another boat built. One last thing, be back within the week whether you have the crown or not. And Brina try to spend part of every day in the water if you can. It will help you remain in human form longer."

"Right," Brina responded, clearly pleased to be chosen to join Ben on this quest.

"Are there any questions before you leave?" Lea Waterborn asked.

"You mean we leave right now?" asked Ben, his voice pitched high.

"Yes," said the Watcher emphatically. "The matter is urgent. The crown must be back in the Mer King's hands before the week is out or there will be a war."

"I don't understand why he would think a hunk of metal is more important than lives," Brina said.

"His pride has been wounded. He will keep his own sons and daughters away from the battle. Those close to him will make sure that no heartbroken mother or father gets too near to disturb him with their tears. It will seem like nothing more than a game to King Somos and his closest supporters."

Lea Waterborn stood and led the way. They stopped briefly at the pool where Akca and Osch waited. The Watcher gave them last minute instructions in their language before they disappeared from sight.

"It will be good to have you with me, Brina," Ben said fervently. He did not want to be alone with Akca and Osch in a world full of water.

The Watcher led them through the corridors that Charla and Ben had traveled the day before. When they emerged from the cave the orcas were by the steps. The orcas were both outfitted with a harness that would hold the boys in place on their backs. A student stood waiting beside the steps with a small backpack in each hand. Attached to each backpack was a short spear.

"Inside your pack there is a small amount of food. Fish should be your diet as long as it is available. The food should be saved for when the journey takes you to land, where there may not be food available."

The student handed a backpack to each of the boys. He also handed Ben a leather knife belt. Ben buckled it around his waist. Brina already had one like it around his own waist. Brina climbed on Osch's back and strapped himself in. Akca waited for Ben to climb on, but Ben stood frozen to the spot.

Ben tried to move his feet forward but they would not work at his command. His mind came up with many different excuses to get him out of this situation. He spoke none of them aloud. Lea Waterborn, Brina, Osch, and Akca were all staring at him. He made his right foot move and then his left. His body was visibly shaking by the time he put a leg over Akca. Ben's hands were shaking so badly that it was hard to strap himself in. Ben shut his eyes and clamped his mouth shut to keep from yelling, "Wait! Stop! I've changed my mind."

CHAPTER SEVEN

LEA WATERBORN

The Watcher shook her head when she saw Ben's fear and wondered, not for the first time, if the Guardian had indeed made a mistake in choosing Ben.

Lea Waterborn had serious concerns about sending the two boys to Spencer Island. It had a well-earned reputation as a dangerous place. Brina was well aware of the dangers. The Watcher had made sure of that. Lea hoped that the knowledge she had shared with Brina would provide the protection needed to bring Brina safely home and send Ben back to his own world.

It was not just what Lea Waterborn knew of the Island that caused her concern, but it was also what she did not know. She did not understand why her connection with the island was lost. Lea Waterborn had agonized over whether to send them into unknown danger, but in the end decided that the Guardian knew Ben's abilities and the situation he was going into.

As Ben and Brina rode out of sight, the Watcher muttered to herself, "I wonder if I should have told them about the rumors. I can't see how they can be true and yet something strange is going on. Something is causing the Tregs to behave in an unnatural way."

One thing Lea Waterborn had kept from Brina was the rumor that a dragon had been seen several times in the sky above the island.

Lea Waterborn assured herself that there could not be a dragon. If there was a dragon, an inexperienced boy would not have been chosen by the Guardian. The Guardian would have sent someone with experience, preferably someone from Zargon who was dragonborn. But perhaps there was no one from Zargon to send. Lea Waterborn had not seen anyone from that world for a long time, and she had lost her connection with the Zargonian Watcher.

The Watchers of each world had a connection with one another through the Guardian of the Six Worlds and they were able to receive impressions and thoughts though this connection when they opened their minds to one another. Through her connection with the Watcher of Earth she sensed Mariah Templeton's anxiety for Ben. She could normally sense each of the other Watchers if she chose to, but now the Watcher of Zargon seemed to be missing from his post. Something was not right on Zargon. However, even if things were not right on Zargon, a dragon could not have come through the portals without her knowledge.

"No," the Watcher muttered as if trying to convince herself, "The Guardian would not have sent an inexperienced boy if there was a dragon. Certainly not!"

She stood watching the two boys ride off until they could no longer be seen. Lea Waterborn felt more anxiety than she had ever known in her three hundred years as the Watcher of Lushaka. Her anxiety kept her from noticing that another pair of eyes watched as well. When the boys were out of sight, Lea Waterborn turned and walked slowly back to her office. It was not until later in the day that she sensed that Charla was absent from Fairwaters.

CHAPTER EIGHT

A CHANGE IN PLANS

Osch and Akca swam side by side. The orca conversed with one another and sometimes with Brina in their high pitched whistles. As the day wore on Ben and Brina had ample opportunity to share the story of their lives and discuss their respective worlds. Ben learned that land was rare on Lushaka. There were isolated islands, but few humans lived on them. Most lived on the lily pads and in the trees that grew up from the bottom of the sea. They even raised livestock on the lily pads, feeding them with sea grasses.

Ben learned that up to fifty years ago Fairwaters had human as well as mer students. A war in the world outside Fairwaters, between mer and humans, divided the students. Most of the mer and all of the humans were expelled from the school.

While almost every other student was the child of parents with the ability to transform, Brina was the son of non-transformers. When he was young, his mother had taken him to see a nearby Island. Brina was fascinated by what he could see and reached out to touch a flower just beyond his reach. Brina was unaware as he did so that his tail disappeared, to be replaced by two very human legs. His mother cried all the way home. She never took her young son near land again. Over the next year she made some discreet inquiries that led to Brina's enrollment in Fairwaters.

Brina and Ben stopped about midday and rested atop a cork lily pad that floated on the water. Akca and Osch disappeared. They soon returned with fish, which they tossed onto the lily pad at Brina's feet. Brina took out a knife and filleted one of the fish, which he held out to Ben. Ben just stared at it.

"Don't you want it?" Brina asked.

"What for?" asked Ben.

"To eat, of course," Brina replied. "Don't you eat fish on your world?"

"Yes, but not raw...at least I don't eat it raw," said Ben.

"Suit yourself," Brina replied as he bit into the raw fish. Ben rooted around in his backpack for something to eat. There were eggs and dried sea cucumbers wrapped in seaweed. Ben ate two eggs. He was about to eat another, when Brina said, "Lea Waterborn told us to save the food she gave us for when we are on land."

Ben wrapped the remaining eggs in the seaweed and returned them to his backpack.

After eating, they climbed aboard Akca and Osch and resumed their trip. In the afternoon they saw tregs more frequently than they had in the morning. Ben guessed that was because they were getting closer to the island where the birds nested. Twice they had to dive down to avoid the tregs. The second time it was a close call and Ben heard the bird shriek in frustration as the orcas dove under water, taking Brina and a terrified Ben with them. The treg's shriek of frustration sent chills deep into Ben's bones.

The treg's third attack came from directly behind and caught them completely by surprise. Brina was the lighter of the two, and it was Brina the treg chose. The bird tried to lift the mer up and carry him away, but Brina was attached to Osch. The bird could not lift the combined weight of Brina and Osch, yet it was unwilling to let go.

Brina tried to pull his knife out from the belt around his waist, but the harness connecting him to Osch broke, and the knife got tangled in it. Ben sat helpless, wanting to do something, but not knowing what he could do as he had no way to communicate with Akca and tell the orca to move closer to Brina and the treg. So he screamed at the bird as Akca swam in circles. The treg lifted a struggling Brina up into the air. The bird's triumphant shriek mingled with Brina's terrified cry.

Osch and Akca whistled loudly and swam around in tight circles. Ben was afraid his harness was going to break with the strain. As he struggled to keep his balance, Ben tried to follow Brina with his eyes as the treg carried him off into the horizon. The orcas finally stopped circling and began to talk with one another in their language. They came to an agreement and turned and began to go back the way they had come.

"No," Ben yelled. The orcas stopped. Ben tried to explain what he wanted. He wanted Akca and Osch to follow Brina, but he was not sure how much they understood. They listened attentively and then started to swim back the way they had come.

They had no sooner got started for the second time when a voice that was not Ben's yelled out, "No!"

It was Charla. Like Ben, she had a small pack with a short spear strapped to her back. Charla began to speak rapidly to the orcas in their language. They argued back and forth and then came to an understanding. Charla turned to Ben. "It is settled," she said. "Osch will go tell Lea Waterborn what happened. Akca will carry you to the human community and leave you where someone is sure to find you. I will follow Brina."

"No. I want to go after Brina," said Ben. "And besides, Lea Waterborn said to stay away from the humans."

"That was before Brina was taken. The best place for you now is with other humans. A human alone on the sea with a war about to break out is not very safe. Someone better suited will be sent to help us get the crown back, and when things settle down you can be found and sent back to earth. If the Guardian does not send someone then Lea Waterborn will have to send some of our own people, which is what should have happened in the first place."

"Lea Waterborn does not know you are here, does she?" Ben asked.

"That is not your concern."

"You should go back to Fairwaters."

"I'm not going back. Osch will tell Lea Waterborn what happened. I am going to rescue Brina."

"I should go with you then," Ben said.

"There are two problems with that. First, I don't want or need your help; and second, Akca wants to get rid of you as soon as possible. He was all for leaving you here, but I convinced him that Lea Waterborn would appreciate it if he took you to the human community."

Charla did not look at Ben as she spoke. The way Charla avoided looking at him and something in the tone of her voice led Ben to think the mermaid was not telling him the truth, but he had no way of talking directly to the orcas. He started to argue, but thought better of it. All he could see was water in every direction. The thought of being left here with nothing to keep him afloat was terrifying. Ben's fear of water pushed every other thought from his mind.

Osch went one way, Charla another, and Akca and Ben traveled towards the human community. When it got dark Akca was to take Ben to a lily pad near the human settlement so that the humans could find him in the morning.

Akca swam quickly, too quickly. It seemed like he did want to be rid of the burden on his back as soon as possible. Akca and Ben arrived on the outskirts of the human community just as the sun was sinking out of sight. It was not dark enough.

Ben knew they were close when enormous trees could be seen off in the distance. The trees were some of the biggest Ben had ever seen. As they drew nearer there was other plant life: grasses, seaweed, and cork lily pads, all with roots deep in the sea. Brina had told Ben that several families could live in the branches of the largest trees. He did not find it difficult to believe as they drew ever closer.

Akca headed for a lily pad on the other side of two small trees. He was just past the trees when disaster struck. Something heavy came down around the two of them. A voice somewhere above yelled, "Here! Come quick! Jared and I have something. I think we've caught a mer."

Akca dove down into the water. He had to make his escape quickly. The humans had thrown a net over them. Weights on the outer edges made it sink down when it was thrown. As soon as the net was thrown a rope was pulled, closing the bottom of the net. Akca might have escaped, had Ben not been strapped to his back. The extra weight slowed him down.

Ben fumbled to find the release on the harness. When he finally found it, the harness came off Akca and fell through the shrinking hole at the bottom of the net. Ben bobbed up to the surface and grabbed one of the buoys that kept the net from sinking. Akca sought to escape through the closing net, but it was too late. The net had been drawn tight and there was no escape.

"Let's see what we have here," Ratore, a young muscular man said.

Hand over hand three humans pulled the net towards them. Ben did not try to talk. He had enough trouble just holding onto the buoy and keeping his head above water as the net was dragged in. The part of the net Ben was tangled in reached the cork lily pad and the three humans pulled him onto it.

"This ain't no mer. It has legs," said Harbo, an older man with a receding hairline.

"I tell you, I saw a fish tail," Ratore stated firmly.

"Jared, bring the lamp so we can see what we have here," Harbo instructed.

Jared, a boy about Ben's age, brought a lamp and held it up so that the three humans could get a good look at Ben.

"I swear I saw a fish tail," Ratore said. "Maybe we've caught ourselves a changeling." Ratore's voice became very harsh and he appeared ready to strike Ben with an oar he picked up.

Ben choked out the words, "not…a…changeling."

"There's something else in the net," Jared piped in.

"Pull it in," said Harbo. "Let's find out what it is."

They left Ben tangled in the net as they dragged the rest of it up onto the lily pad.

"See, what did I tell you?" Ratore said, as they dragged the struggling orca out of the water, "A mer fish friend. We have caught a changeling." Ratore appeared ready to bash Ben's brains out with the oar he held in his hands.

"I'm not a changeling!" Ben said. Ben knew from the tone in Ratore's voice that a changeling was not a good thing to be in the present company.

"That's for the council to decide," Harbo said firmly.

Ben started to explain who he was. "I am…" Ben began, but then hesitated.

I am a chosen sent to this world from another. Yeah, right. He wasn't sure he believed that. I came through a door that links your world to mine. Definitely, not believable.

The two men and the boy stared down at him. Their faces showed their growing suspicion.

Akca flopped about in the net and made a high pitched squealing sound.

"Tell your fish friend to be quiet or we'll cut his throat here and now," Ratore said. "At least we'll eat well tonight."

Akca either understood what was said or guessed by the note of threat in Ratore's voice. He was quiet and stopped flopping.

Harbo grunted and cleared his throat. "We have never eaten the mer fish friends before. It is part of the agreement between the mer and us. However, tonight, the council might make an exception. Food is becoming scarce. There are some hungry people in our Treehold.

All of us will soon be starving if that crown is not found and returned."

Ratore tied Ben's hands and feet none too gently while Harbo untangled him from the net. Ratore tied a rope around Akca's snout, but left the orca in the net. Jared brought over a large canoe shaped boat. Ratore and Harbo dragged the net into the boat. It was not an easy task. The orca weighed at least three hundred pounds. As Jared held the boat steady, they dumped Akca into the bottom of it. Ratore and Harbo picked Ben up and threw him in on top of Akca.

They had not traveled far when the sound of humans living together was heard. There was talking and laugher, arguments and tears, children playing and people working. The same kind of sounds can be heard when you walk down an Earthen street on a hot summer day.

The boat bumped up against something solid and Jared jumped out. He tied the boat and steadied it as Harbo rolled Ben out of the boat onto a lily pad. Ratore and Harbo dragged Akca out of the boat and left the orca on the lily pad tangled in the net.

"Ratore, you and I will take the stranger to the council," said Harbo. "Jared will stay here and guard the mer friend."

"There's no point in carrying the changeling when he has two good legs," said Ratore. He used a knife to cut the rope around Ben's legs. He was none too careful and a line of blood appeared on Ben's left leg. Ben bit his lip and glared at Ratore.

Jared and Harbo stood Ben up. Ben had longed to have something solid under his feet, but now found that his legs would not hold him up. He'd been in the water a long time, with little to eat since breakfast. But to be honest, it was partly fear that made Ben's legs weak. What was he going to say to this council to convince them that he was not a changeling?"

As Harbo and Ratore led Ben away he looked over his shoulder at Akca. The orca was clearly in distress. Obviously he could not stay out of the water long.

"Akca needs to be in the water," Ben said. "He might die if you leave him there."

As soon as the words were out of his mouth Ben knew they were a mistake. He had just convinced the three humans that he was a traitor or a changeling. He knew the orca by name.

"Good!" Ratore said. "We'll eat tonight then. In fact if the fish doesn't die on its own, I might help it on its way. How do you like that Changeling?" Ratore punched Ben on the shoulder. Ben stumbled and fell. Tears came to Ben's eyes as he gasped in pain. Harbo shook his head and helped Ben up.

"Ratore, run ahead and ring the bell to call the council to convene," Harbo instructed. I can handle this boy alone." Harbo gave Ratore a meaningful look that communicated that he did not approve of the muscular Ratore beating up on someone weaker.

Ratore sprinted up the six steps that led up from the lily pad to a walkway made of wooden slats. Harbo followed and led Ben along the swaying walkway. Harbo held onto Ben's arm, which helped Ben keep his balance. There was a rope available for that purpose, but Ben could not hold it as he hands were still tied.

By now, the sun was gone. A large moon hung low in the sky. A second moon was rising out of the east. Together, the two moons gave enough light to see the path. Ben could see that several paths intersected the one they were on. From the trees Ben could hear the murmur of voices. Occasionally a soft glow filtered down through the branches.

Harbo and Ben had just turned to the right when a bell rang. They made two more turns before they reached a path with an upward slope. Dark shapes moved ahead of them, behind them, and along the other paths that converged at the meeting hall. In front of them light shone through the branches of trees. They passed between two tall trees and arrived at a large platform that was covered by a roof. A wall went as far up as a grown man's waist. From the top of the wall to the roof the meeting place was open. The roof was supported by trees, as was the platform on which they stood. There was a door on each of the four sides of the platform. People streamed through each door and were filling the benches that went around three sides of the meeting place. There was a row of nine chairs at the front, where people had gathered and were talking to Ratore. Harbo pushed Ben towards them. When they arrived at the front of the hall, the nine community elders took their seats and Ben stood before them with Ratore on one side of him and Harbo on the other side.

CHAPTER NINE

TO TELL THE TRUTH

"You have called the council together. What reason do you give?" a short plump man with a fringe of hair around his bald head intoned. All eyes were on Ben as these words were spoken. They were a formality. Everyone knew Ben was the reason the council had been called.

"Ratore, Jared, and I were fishing on the outskirts of our village," Harbo said. "We fished all day and caught almost nothing. We decided to stay out longer than normal. Ratore and Jared heard something. They threw their net. In it we caught this boy. He was in the company of a mer companion fish."

At these words murmurs arose from those sitting in the benches.

"I think we caught a changeling spy," Ratore said loudly. "Why else would a fish bring him here as it grows dark?"

The murmurs grew louder. Words of affirmation could be heard in the crowd.

The man who had spoken earlier looked at Ben, "What is your name and what do you have to say for yourself?"

"My name is Benjamin Taylor and I'm not a changeling spy. What I am is shipwrecked and lost. The orca, and orcas are not fish but mammals because they breathe air, decided to help me for some reason."

"We don't know anything about orcas or care how they breathe, we want to know why a mer companion fish would help a human on the eve of a war?" an elder asked.

"I have no idea," Ben said.

Ratore interjected, "He knows the fish by name. I heard him call it Akca. How would he know the fish by name if he were not really a mer who only appears human?"

The murmur from the benches grew louder. "A changeling!" Voices throughout the meeting hall began to call for Ben's death.

For a moment the council leader said nothing. "Let's hear from the boy himself. How do you know the name of the fish?" he asked.

Ben groaned. Akca had not looked well when they left him. If something was not decided soon the Akca would die.

"I will tell you everything after you let Akca go," Ben said. "Akca needs to be back in the water soon or he will die."

"The fish will not be going anywhere until we find out who you are and what you are doing here," responded the man. "Then, we'll see. You haven't told us how you know this fish by name?"

Ben should have known that he'd have to answer questions, which meant he was in trouble as he'd never been a good liar. What could he possibly tell the council that they would believe? Finally, Ben settled on the truth, "I have come from another world. I was sent here to help you recover the crown so that a war with the mer can be averted."

At that the whole group did exactly what Ben thought they would do. They did what he would have done in their shoes. They laughed.

"I think we've caught a turtle with a cracked shell," a voice said. "Maybe he's been out in the sun too long."

"Maybe he was sent away from his own Treehold because he caused too much trouble with his wild stories and lies," one of the council members said. There was a lot of agreement in the gathering place.

"It could be that he is a criminal trying to escape punishment in his own Treehold," another council leader said. "But I think it is more likely that he is a changeling come to spy on us. Otherwise, why would he arrive at night? Whatever this Benjamin Taylor is, I intend to find out even if it takes all night."

Ben thought of how he disappeared in Miss Templeton's office and wished he could do that now. There was a collective gasp as his wish was granted. Then everyone started talking at once.

"Quiet everyone!" the council leader yelled. "Guard the exits! Quick!"

Ben stepped back from where he stood between Harbo and Ratore and then stepped sideways. He stepped forward through two council members and stood behind the now vacant row of chairs as people ran to each of the three doors. People milled around the meeting room, checking under benches and in corners and behind chairs. Ben stood close to the council leader's chair and used his teeth to loosen the knotted rope around his wrists. It would have been easier if he could see his wrists and the rope that held them tight. However, he was invisible not only to others, but also to himself. Twice he had to move to avoid a searcher.

"What kind of trick is this?" said a voice beside Ben. "He has disappeared. He's not here." Ben sidled away and slipped between two chairs.

"Perhaps he's gone to rescue his fish friend," said the leader of the council. "Harbo will stay here to tell us everything that happened." The leader pointed to two men, "You two go with Ratore. Guard the orca in case the outsider tries to help his fish friend. The rest of you fan out and search the entire community. When the outsider is found we will ring the bell and gather back here."

When Ratore left, Ben followed them. He knew that he would never find his own way back to where Akca was in the dark; maybe not even in daylight. The village was a warren of paths that led every which way. Ben gave up trying to get the rope off with his teeth. It was hard enough to keep his balance on the swaying walkway. He resumed working on the knot when they arrived at the cork pad where

Akca was in clear distress. Ben stood on the walkway above the steps and watched the three Lushakan humans he had been following go down to the lily pad to talk to Jared.

"The outsider has escaped. Have you seen him?" Ratore asked.

"I haven't seen anyone," said Jared. "How did he get away?"

"He disappeared from the meeting place. One minute he was there and the next, he was gone. We all had our eyes on him the whole time he was there. I've never seen anything like it. I'd sure like to know how he did it."

"He's not here," Jared said, looking around. "At least, I don't think he is."

"He was real concerned about this fish and I think he might want to help it," Ratore said.

"He was right about the mer fish friend," Jared said. "It's not doing so well. It needs to be in water. Did the council say anything about it? Can we release it now?" There was a note of hope in the last question.

"We never got a chance to discuss the companion fish before the stranger disappeared," a man named Sueska responded.

"I think we should let it go," Jared said, his voice pleading.

"I think we should kill it right now," said Ratore. "The council would be happy to be spared the problem of making a decision." Ratore stepped forward menacingly. Jared stepped between him and Akca.

"Ratore has a point," Sueska said. "The council will not make this decision easily. By the time they do the fish will likely be dead. Its death now would not be a bad thing. Rations are short now and that will only get worse if there is a war. Who knows, we might acquire a taste for the companion fish."

"But they are different. They can talk," Jared protested.

"They have never talked to me," Ratore said "Have they ever talked to anyone else here?" There was silence. "Well, have you ever had them talk to you Jared?"

"No, but…"

"Perhaps they really can't talk. We only have the word of the mer for that, and their word can't be trusted."

"But, but…we have an agreement not to eat mer fish friends."

"In times of war, agreements no longer hold," Sueska said.

From behind Ben, a voice called out, "Have you seen the stranger? Has he come back here?"

Ben had a problem. Two people were walking towards him. They could not help but run into him if he stayed where he was. They were walking side by side on the narrow walkway. Sueska and his companions stood at the bottom of the steps in such a way that Ben could not slip by them onto the lily pad.

Ben had made progress in undoing the rope around his wrists. He bent his head and pulled frantically with his teeth. The two searchers were close enough to touch Ben when the rope slid from his hands. The rope became visible as it fell to the ground.

"Did you see that?" one of the men demanded. "That rope came out of nowhere. The changeling must be close by."

The group took another step forward. Ben took the only option available to him. He stepped off the walkway into the water. Ben found himself once more in water over his head. He went under briefly, but quickly surfaced.

Above Ben a voice shouted, "What was that?"

Ben looked up. Two men were staring down at him. Ben was still invisible, but they could see the unusual hole in the water where Ben's body was.

"Something's down there," Sueska said. "Take a couple of boats and investigate."

Ratore and three of the other men took two of the boats out, which left only Sueska and Jared on the lily pad.

Ben knew he needed to get out of the water before a boat came around beside him. They might not be able to see him, but they would be able to see where he was as long as he was in the water. Ben's attempts to swim had always been accompanied by a great deal of splashing as he thrashed about in the water. This time he gently kicked his legs and slowly moved his arms out into the water and back towards himself. It was the first time he had tried such a movement and it was surprisingly successful. He moved towards an upright log that supported the walkway. Once there he thought of the suction cups that had helped him stay on Akca's back. They appeared and he climbed the log easily and pulled his invisible self onto the now empty walkway. Ben moved quietly onto the lily pad. It dipped slightly as he stepped onto it, but Jared and Sueska did not notice. Ben walked along the outside of the lily pad on the opposite side of the men searching for him with their boats. Jared and Sueska had their backs to him and did not notice the wet footprints or the water that dripped from him onto the lily pad. He knelt down beside Akca. The orca was barely breathing. It lay unmoving on the lily pad although Jared had untangled it from the net.

Ben took hold of the rope around Akca's snout. To his surprise he found the rope was already untied and had been draped over the orca's jaw to give the appearance that it was still tied. Ben, still invisible, pushed Akca, but the orca was heavy and he was not able to move him. He pushed again and this time it was easier. It was easier because there was another pair of hands pushing. While Sueska faced the other way, watching the boats that were searching for Ben, Jared pushed Akca. As the orca flopped into the water, Jared stood up and yelled, "Help, the fish has escaped."

Ben moved quickly out of the way. He climbed into a boat as the men converged back at the point where Akca had gone into the water. Ratore looked suspiciously at Jared. "How did that fish get untangled from the net?"

"I loosened it," Jared replied. "I didn't think it had the strength to escape."

"You can come with us and explain to the council how that fish escaped." Sueska said firmly. "Tully, you search this area. Kirk, you guard the walkway leading to this pad until you are relieved."

Sueska's command did not sit well with Kirk. "The changeling escaped with his fish friend. He's long gone. There's no need for me to stay and miss the council meeting," he said.

"If Kirk is not staying, neither am I," stated Tully.

"All right," Sueska replied. "Search the area and then come to the meeting hall."

Ben leaned back in the boat and pulled a piece of the sail over himself. After Kirk and Tully finished he planned to take a boat and make his escape. He listened to Tully sing in the darkness as he searched. Ben's eyes closed. The boat rocked gently back and forth in the waves. Ben soon fell asleep. The moment he fell asleep, Ben became visible.

CHAPTER TEN

FRIEND OR FOE

When Ben opened his eyes he expected to see his roommate Denzel. His first thought was that Denzel was beside him, waking him up from a nightmare. When he actually opened his eyes it was not Denzel's dark face he saw, but Jared's round freckled face. Jared's blue eyes were staring down at him. Jared was shaking him awake. Ben became invisible a moment later. So did Jared's hand and arm. Jared's eyes went wide and he gasped. At the same time he tightened his grip on Ben's invisible shoulder.

"The council members will send someone down here soon," Jared said quietly. "I wouldn't want to be you when they get here. I've got one question and I want a true response. Did you really come to find the crown and stop a war between us and the mer?"

Everything in Ben wanted to find a way to leave this world and its endless water, but he whispered, "Yes."

"I'm going to help you escape," said Jared quietly. "In exchange you will do me a favor."

"What favor?" Ben asked.

"Let me come with you." Jared responded.

An invisible Ben quickly whispered, "Yes."

"Do you promise to take me with you?"

"Yes," Ben stated firmly. In truth it would be a relief not to be alone in this strange world.

"I'd stay invisible if I were you. I think everyone is asleep, but it is better to be safe than sorry," Jared said.

A faint glow shone on the eastern horizon with the promise of a new day. One moon hung low in the western sky, the other had disappeared. Jared pushed the boat away from the lily pad and rowed it out into open water where he untied the sail and rigged it out. He took hold of the tiller as a stiff breeze caught the sail.

"I figured you were around somewhere," Jared said. "I tried really hard to get that fish off the pad before the others came. It wouldn't budge. I pushed with all my strength. Couldn't figure out how it got so much easier until I thought about how you disappeared from sight right in front of the whole council. Then I realized you must have been pushing that fish alongside me. I'd sure like you to teach me how to be invisible."

"I'm sorry. I don't think it's something you can teach."

"Yeah…it figures. It's a pity though. Where we are going it would help to be invisible."

"And where's that?"

"Spencer Island. It is where the tregs nest. And from all accounts there are other dangers besides the tregs. People almost never go to Spencer Island and when they do, they almost never return."

"And you want to go there?"

"I have to. That's where my brother is and he needs my help if he's going to come home again. I told the council that and they didn't believe me, just like they didn't believe you when you said you were sent to find the crown. I'm not sure I believe you either. Why would anyone send a kid like you to do such a dangerous job?"

Ben bristled a little at being called a kid by someone just a bit older than he was. "I don't know," he finally said. "It doesn't make sense to me either."

"Who sent you?"

"My school principal, Miss Templeton, but she really didn't want to send me. Someone called the Guardian told her to do it."

"The Guardian?"

"The Guardian is someone or something who watches over six worlds that are somehow linked together. There are doors between the worlds and people like Miss Templeton on Earth and Lea Waterborn on Lushaka train people to send though those doors to other worlds to do the work of this Guardian."

"Which is?"

"Peace, justice, help for people in trouble…I guess. At least that is what I've been able to pick up in the past two days."

Jared snorted and then laughed out loud, "That's an unbelievable story."

"Yeah," Ben said. "I wouldn't believe it either, but here I am, in a world not my own. I tried to convince myself it was a nightmare I'm having trouble waking up from. Perhaps it is."

Ben was silent for several minutes as he thought about all that had happened to him in the past two days. "Your brother is on Spencer Island. Is there anyone else with him?" he finally asked.

"My brother and five others are missing. Four weeks ago, three of our bravest and best went out after that crown. They never returned. Six days ago, another group of three went out including my older brother Gill. I wanted to go, but they wouldn't have me. They said I was too young. Every day that Gill has been gone I have felt dread grow in me. Somehow, I know he can't come back unless I help him."

"Six days isn't that long to be gone," Ben said. "He might be on his way back already."

"He isn't. Like I said, I can't explain it, but I just know that my brother is in trouble and unless I go help him, he will not come home ever. I don't know how I know this. I just do. Every day this feeling that my brother's life depends on me grows stronger. The council is debating whether to send another group of three. By the time they finish debating, my brother will be dead and the war will have begun in earnest."

Ben was silent as he thought about Jared's words. "If your brother could not conquer whatever is on that island," he finally said, "what makes you think that you and I can?"

"Every night for the last week I've had dreams, dreams unlike anything I have ever dreamed before. My dreams show me going to rescue my brother as one of a group of three. Three travel up the mountain. They rescue Gill and bring back the crown."

"There are only two of us."

"My dreams were of three. A rope with three strands is not easily broken. Perhaps a third will show up just like you did. And if not, then the two of us will do what it needs three people to do."

Ben was no longer invisible. Invisibility required that he concentrate some effort on remaining so. As he and Jared talked he had slowly materialized without realizing it. Ben had a sinking feeling that he knew who the third would be if there was any truth to Jared's dreams.

"No way! Not if I can help it!" he muttered to himself. Ben had no desire to spend any more time in Charla's company.

Jared broke into his thoughts, "You really believe you're from another world?"

"Yes!"

"Huh," Jared grunted. Disbelief was clearly written on his face. "Tell me something about Earth."

"It's different from Lushaka. In our world there is only one moon. There are no mer," Ben paused and then said, "at least none that I know of."

"That's an improvement," Jared broke in.

"We have a lot more land than you have," Ben continued. "And we don't live in trees. We build our houses on the land from trees that we cut down."

"You're going to have to come up with a better story than that for anyone to believe you. Why would people live on land? Most of it's dangerous and besides, food comes from the sea."

"It's not a story. Every word is true. My world is different than yours. Most of our food comes from the land rather than the sea." Ben said loudly. He did not like being called a liar.

"Okay, okay, so you come from another world," Jared said soothingly, "where people live on land and you've been chosen by someone called the Guardian to come to Lushaka and help stop a war." Jared's tone suggested that he was not convinced, but didn't think it was worth an argument.

"Tell me about the tregs," Ben said, partly because he wanted to change the subject.

"The tregs around here make Spencer Island their home. From there they fly out over the water looking for food—fish, animals, people, and mer. A full grown adult is normally safe from attack, but we have always had to watch our children. A year ago, the tregs behavior changed. They started to pick up things, things like wood, rope, pots, trinkets, and now the Mer King's crown."

"Why would they do that?" Ben asked.

"No one knows, but a dragon was seen flying near the Island."

"A dragon! What kind of dragon?"

"The only kind there is. As big as a whale, like a lizard, only it flies. And if the stories are true, it can turn you into a lump of charcoal with the fire it breathes."

"Has anyone seen this dragon?" Ben asked.

"Two men of our clan have seen it from a distance."

"Do you believe them?"

Jared shrugged. "The council didn't believe them."

"Ah," Ben said aloud, but he felt quite sure there was no dragon.

The wind was brisk and the boat made rapid progress. At midmorning the island appeared before them. The island was actually a single mountain that rose up out of the sea. A sandy beach stretched along the shore for as far as Ben could see. From the beach to the forest there was about a quarter mile of sand.

Jared brought the sail down as they approached the beach. The boat bumped softly against the shore. Jared jumped into the shallow water and grabbed a rope to pull the boat up onto the dry land. Just as he was going to step onto the sand, a single word rang out, "Stop!"

Jared scanned the shore and then the water. Coming towards them was a mer. Jared grabbed one of the spears from the bottom of the boat.

"It's okay! Put the spear down," Ben said.

But Jared continued to hold the spear over his head in his right hand. Ben jumped into the water, grabbed the spear from Jared and threw it back into the bottom of the boat. Once again the voice, this time closer, yelled out with urgency, "Stop. Don't step onto the sand."

Jared clearly took these words as a threat and once again reached for the spear. Ben grabbed his arm and the two of them struggled until they fell into the water. When they were back on their feet Charla was there with her hand resting on the boat. Jared stepped backwards onto the wet sand of the shoreline. Behind him, in all directions, the sand began to move. The ripples came closer and closer, but Jared was not looking at the sand, he was looking at Charla.

"Don't come any closer Fish Breath, or I'll make you sorry you did!" he yelled.

"You stupid tree ape, look at the sand behind you!" Charla said in a high-pitched voice. Jared thought it was a trick and ignored her, but Ben turned and saw the moving sand. Ben grabbed Jared and dragged him deeper into the water.

Jared fought back and screamed, "Let go of me you changeling traitor." The struggle turned Jared around so that he faced the land. He stopped fighting when he saw the moving sand. From all directions things under the sand converged to where Jared had just been standing. Jared broke free of Ben and dove into the boat. Ben followed him in. Whatever was under the sand moved to where the boat rested on the shore. Jared took a paddle and pushed them away from land. They inspected the sandy beach they had just about walked onto from a safe distance away.

"Bones, there are bones everywhere." Jared murmured.

Not far away was an old skull—either human or mer. A strange-looking creature stared at them through an empty eye socket.

"I came from that direction," Charla pointed. "Back that way there is a recent skull on the beach. There's hair attached to it, with scattered bits of clothing and a weapon. The sand around the skull is dark with what looks like dried blood."

"Was it human or mer?" Jared interrupted.

"Human," Charla replied.

"What color?" Jared asked.

"Dark brown," said Charla.

"Not my brother Gill," Jared murmured, with a sigh of relief.

"I wanted to get a closer look so I went onto the shore," Charla continued. "I reached out my arm to pick up the weapon when there was movement under the sand. I wondered if whatever it was had killed whoever died there. So I caught a fish to throw on the sand and see what happened."

"What happened?" Ben asked.

"I saw you coming. I decided it was more important to warn you and experiment later. Don't you think I made a good choice?" Charla finished smugly.

"Maybe," Ben replied reluctantly. "Let's see."

Charla took the fish out of her net and gave it to Ben. "Throw it up onto the beach," she directed.

There was no sign of movement as Ben stood and tossed the fish up onto the dry land. Almost immediately the sand began to bubble and churn. Things under the sand were moving towards the fish. Creatures with hard shells that reminded Ben of clams popped out from under the sand. The idea that these creatures looked like clams evaporated the moment lids on two bumps at the top front of each shell rolled back to reveal a pair of beady eyes. Supporting the shell was a set of eight armor-coated legs. The lower front of the shell cracked open to reveal a bird-like beak. The beak contained razor sharp teeth. The creatures looked like a cross between a clam, a spider, a bird, and a rabid dog. The beak and teeth were in constant motion. Ben, Jared and Charla watched in horror as hundreds of the creatures fought over the fish. More were arriving all the time.

The latecomers found nothing to devour, so they attacked their brothers and sisters who had arrived before them. They tore off one another's legs. They broke open the shell of their crippled brothers and sisters and ate what was inside. The spider clams that were still whole, and not cannibalizing one of their own, popped back under the sand. Some turned and ran at the two humans and the mermaid. The boys took their oars and pushed further back out to sea. However they need not have feared for each wave sent the creatures scrambling back to dry land. They did not like water. There were maybe a dozen clams that had lost too many legs to dig into the sand and disappear. One of them was happily eating what remained of his brother's leg without realizing that every one of his own legs was gone. Ben, Jared, and Charla looked across the expanse of sand and saw the bleached bones of a dozen creatures both big and small.

Jared shuddered, "That could have been me. I would have walked right into the middle of them if you hadn't stopped me. They would have hamstrung me and when I lay helpless they would have eaten the eyeballs right out of my head. They would have eaten bits and pieces while I was still alive. Pfeww! I owe you my life. If your life is ever in danger call on me. I am duty bound to help you. My name is Jared Trentarry."

"You were lucky that I was here and decided to help a tree ape," Charla said, the last words spoken with distain.

"Are you alone? Are there other mer with you?" Jared scanned the sea anxiously.

"I'm here alone," Charla said.

Relief could be clearly seen on Jared's face.

"I am able to take care of myself," Charla said. "And just so we are clear, I will never want help from you!"

"Is this where the treg brought Brina?" Ben asked Charla.

"Brina?" Jared grunted.

Charla ignored Jared and answered Ben's question, "Yes, I think so. The treg was flying this way. Which makes sense as this is where the tregs nest."

"You...know each other," Jared said incredulously. Turning to Ben he said, "You are a changeling traitor. Get out of my boat."

"Jared, I'm not a changeling or a traitor, and I'm not getting out of this boat. Brina and Charla are students at the school I told you about here on Lushaka."

"You told this tree ape about the school," Charla exclaimed. "You ought not to have done that."

Ben ignored the mer girl and told Jared how he met Charla and her friend Brina and how Brina had been chosen to help him find the crown and prevent the war. He told of how Brina had been picked up by a Treg. Ben left out any mention of Brina being in human form at the time.

Jared did not seem very satisfied with the explanation; however, he let the matter drop.

"A lot of good a mer was going to be in getting that crown back," Jared said. "The tregs nest at the top of the mountain and that is where they take their loot."

"We need to travel along the shore and see if there is a way to get to the forest without walking on sand," Ben said. "With any luck those creatures live only in sand."

"Perhaps there are places with solid rock," Jared said.

"A river we can travel up might take us past the sand," Charla added.

"There is no we," Jared said. "You can't come where we are going.

In response, Charla disappeared under the water with a slap of her tail. The water splashed into the boat and soaked both Ben and Jared.

CHAPTER ELEVEN

DIE ANOTHER DAY

They sailed up the coast and around the tip of the Island without seeing a break in the sand. Charla accompanied the boat as it sailed. It was late afternoon before they found a stream that emptied into the sea. Jared took down the sails, and picked up an oar. He gave a second oar to Ben. They sat together on the middle bench and rowed up the stream.

Charla led the way. The spider clams popped out and gathered on the banks of both sides of the stream, like a crowd gathered for a parade. Their razor sharp teeth ground back and forth as they hopped up and down on their eight legs. The sound of their grinding teeth sent chills down Ben's spine.

Ben had not handled an oar very often in his life. His oar went wide and came close to shore. The first time it got too close three of the sand creatures hopped onto it and ran towards Ben's hands. His scream alerted Jared, who knocked them into the water.

"Keep your oar close to the boat," Jared yelled.

Ben grunted and tried to do what Jared suggested. The sand creatures continued to gather. At first there were hundreds and then there were thousands. The sound of their grinding teeth made it difficult to carry on a conversation.

They moved closer to the forest as they rowed. As they drew near the occasional solitary tree stood alone with its roots in the sandy beach that rimmed the island. One of the solitary trees had fallen partly into the water, half of it submerged. On the part that was out of water, spider clams danced. There was a narrow gap between the submerged tree and the sandy riverbank where a boat could get through. Sand creatures fought with one another to be the closest to the boat when it went through the gap. They knocked several of their number into the water, where they sank like a stone. As the boat squeezed through the narrow passage some jumped for the boat, missed and sank out of sight. A significant number managed to land inside the boat.

Jared turned quickly to face the opposite direction to Ben so that their backs were to one another. The boys used the oars to knock the sand creatures off the boat. At the same time they tried to keep the boat from being pushed closer to shore by the current. A sudden intense pain caused Ben to look down. A spider clam was attached to his leg. He grabbed it by the shell, pried it off, and threw it overboard where it quickly sank out of sight. Another was climbing up Ben's leg. He picked it off and threw it after the first one. Jared screamed in pain and a third spider clam followed the two Ben had thrown overboard.

Meanwhile a horde of spider clams came from every direction, drawn by the scent of blood. A steady stream jumped from the log to the boat, which was beginning to drift backwards to the sea. Charla grabbed the rope at the front of the boat and used it to pull them upstream.

"This is impossible!" Ben yelled. "Push us back to sea."

"No, we must keep going!" Jared shouted. "Help me, Ben!"

Ben turned to see that the back of the boat was full of sand creatures. They covered the fish net that lay on the bottom of the boat. They were attracted by the smell of previous catches and were chewing on the net. Jared was trying to lift the heavy clam-laden net overboard without getting his fingers taken off. Ben jumped over the seat and together they picked the net up and tossed it over the side. The sand creatures climbed on top of one another to avoid contact with the water as the net sank. It reminded Ben of a King of the Castle game he had played on a pile of snow.

Ben jumped back over the seat to battle spider clams at the front of the boat. Five of them ran at him and bit into his leg. Thankfully, his pants provided some protection, but it was still very painful. He ripped one after another off his leg and threw them overboard until there were no more in the boat. Another boat was directly ahead of them, moored in midstream. Beyond the boat was a large tree that had fallen across the stream and blocked any further movement upstream by boat. Jumping up and down on the tree were thousands of spider clams. Ben sat down and closed his eyes.

"What are we going to do?" Ben said flatly. "I don't see how we can go any further. There is no getting past that tree."

"We can start by mooring the boat." Jared said. "Charla, I will put out the anchor. Can you tie this boat to the other one and make sure they are both secure? I would hate to come back and find my boat has gone back to sea."

"At least I know my brother made it this far. That's his boat," Jared said when Charla was gone.

Charla popped up beside them, "The boat is secure."

"Thanks," Jared said. "Now, can you go upstream and investigate? See how far the sand continues and whether there is any sign of spider clams past the sand."

Charla disappeared, and Jared and Ben sat in silence watching the hungry would-be diners jumping up and down on the fallen log as they anticipated their next meal.

Charla surfaced in the water beside the boat. "The sand disappears almost immediately beyond this tree," she said. "The water is deep right here. It is possible to swim underwater and get past the sand creatures. After that it becomes shallower."

"I can't swim underwater," Ben said.

"Yes, you can," replied Charla. "You hold your breath, and I will hold you and make sure you stay underwater. You kick your feet and together we'll swim."

Ben sat there and said nothing.

"You can't stay here!" Jared said loudly. "There is no way back and the only way forward is underwater. It's an easy enough thing to do."

"Easy for you maybe!" said Ben stubbornly. Ben was silent for a moment. "But as you say, there is no other way."

Jared picked up his pack and one of the spears on the bottom of the boat and jumped into the water without hesitation. Ben tentatively climbed out of the boat. Once in the water he clung to the boat, unwilling to let it go. When Charla came alongside and took one hand, he still had a hard time letting go. Charla flipped her tail and dragged Ben away. As Ben struggled, she towed him underwater to the other side of the fallen tree. She continued to tow him until the water was shallow enough for Ben to walk. The shoreline turned to rock and the sand creatures disappeared. Ben and Jared left the water and took a trail that ran alongside the stream. Charla followed them upstream in the water until they reached a waterfall.

The sun hung low in the horizon and it was growing dark under the canopy of trees. Charla sat on a partly submerged rock near the bank of the river with her tail in the water.

"Thanks for your help," Jared said to Charla. "We would have had a hard time getting this far without you. I will remember your help if we meet again."

"I don't think we should go further today," Charla said, ignoring Jared. "This looks like a good place to spend the night."

"What do you mean we?" Ben asked.

"I'm going with you," Charla said.

"I don't think that's a good idea," Ben said.

"As if the mermaid could come with us," Jared snorted. "We can't carry you up the mountain and you can't swim past that waterfall. The only way you could come is if you sprout wings!"

"Will legs do?" Charla said as her tail transformed.

Faster than Ben could blink, Jared's spear was headed for Charla's chest. Ben grabbed hold of the spear and threw it into the bush. Jared took out his knife. Ben grabbed the arm that held the knife.

"Whatever happened to 'I owe you my life and I'm duty bound to help you?'" Ben asked hotly.

"That was before I knew she was a changeling. My first duty is to my people. I am duty bound to kill a changeling before it comes among our people to betray us. Every…" Whatever else Jared had planned to say, was cut short by a spear that Charla pointed at Jared's neck. There was a trickle of blood where Charla's spear tip rested.

"Go ahead tree ape," Charla hissed through clenched teeth, "try to plunge your knife into me. I will kill you first."

Jared's arm fell. "I will not kill you today, for you have saved my life this day. However, you had better do what your traitor friend said and go back to where you came from. Otherwise I cannot guarantee your life. If I do not kill you, my brother or one of the other men from my village will."

"I'm going with you," Charla said firmly.

"Charla! That's not a good idea. Lea Waterborn would not approve."

"I'm going. You cannot stop me," Charla stubbornly repeated. "I will go on my own if I have to, but we should go together. Three together will have a better chance to survive this island than one alone. A threefold cord is not easily broken."

"Charla, we cannot stop you, but I think you should go back," Ben said. Charla did not reply. It was clear that she had no intention of returning to Fairwaters without Brina and the crown.

Jared said nothing, but it was clear that he wanted nothing to do with a changeling.

"Well Jared, your dream said three would go."

"But I never dreamed a mer changeling would be one of the three. We can't trust her. She will betray us."

"I don't like this any better than you do, Jared, however, I have enough experience with Charla to know that she will try to go on her own if we do not let her come with us. Who knows, maybe we'll be glad to have her along." Ben said these last words without conviction. He could not imagine ever being happy for the mermaid's company. "Jared, you must promise not to harm Charla if you want to come with me," Ben concluded.

Jared paused briefly, before responding, "I promise before the Creator of all Worlds, and in the name of my honored ancestors to be true to my word. I, Jared, son of Minro, son of Jared, son of Petra, son of Gill, will do everything I can to protect and prolong the life of Charla, mer changeling, at least until we have found the crown and rescued my brother. So I have vowed and so I will do. If it is not so, may I be cut off from my ancestors in that place beyond death, and may my name be forgotten among my people."

"Well," Ben breathed, clearly taken aback by Jared's vow. "Just one more thing. You need to extend that agreement till Charla is back in the sea."

"Agreed," Jared responded.

"Charla, I want your promise that you will do nothing to hurt Jared," Ben said, "or I will go with Jared and you will be left alone."

The mermaid nodded reluctantly. "I will do no harm to this tree ape."

"Then it is settled. Put away your weapons," Ben commanded.

Jared returned his knife to its sheath and went to look for his spear. Charla slid her spear into its holder. Relief flooded through Ben. His hands shook. His legs felt weak. Ben knelt down on the ground. He leaned forward with his eyes closed. When he opened his eyes, Ben saw footprints.

"Someone came this way," Ben said, his voice shaking.

"It was my brother Gill," Jared said with conviction.

"I may be able to follow the trail. It is one of the strange things they teach us at school."

"I will catch some fish for our supper," Charla said. Charla's words brought a smile to Jared's face that was quickly replaced by a scowl as Charla resumed her fish tail and disappeared into the small pond below the waterfall.

"I don't suppose you have matches?" Ben asked.

"What are matches?" Jared asked.

"I was afraid you might say that," Ben said.

"Well, what are matches?"

"Something to start a fire with," Ben responded.

"I have fire rocks. But fish is just as good raw as it is cooked. And a fire might draw the attention of a treg or some other creature."

Their conversation ended with Charla's return. She threw a fat fish on the shore before disappearing into the water again. Jared had the first fish filleted when Charla came back with a second. He handed the first one to Ben. Ben stared at it, completely turned off by the idea of eating raw fish. He sat there holding the raw fish in his hands as Jared and then Charla ate with obvious enjoyment.

"You had better eat up," Jared said. You can't climb mountains without food in your belly."

Ben bit into the fish and discovered that it was not nearly as bad as he imagined it would be. In fact it was really very good.

"I'll be lying in the stream, close by that rock if you need me," Charla said after the meal was over.

When Charla lay in the stream, Ben noticed for the first time that Charla had gills just behind her ears, which slowly moved in and out. He walked over to a patch of grass under a tree and lay down. Jared joined him. Before long they were both fast asleep.

Above Charla's head was something she had never seen before. "How beautiful," she murmured.

There was a circular pattern made of thread suspended between two trees. Thick lines of thread went from a center point to the outer edges. Other lines crossed these lines in circles that became ever closer to one another as they went towards the center. Ben could have told Charla what it was, but as a creature of the sea she did not know. Charla's eyes closed and she never saw the bird fly into the thread and become entangled. She also never saw the creature that came out to feed on it.

CHAPTER TWELVE

CHARLA TO THE RESCUE

Charla was having a bad dream. Her hands were clenched. Her tail thrashed back and forth. Her head moved from side to side. In her dream, Brina and Jared were up a tree surrounded by sand. Jared was trying to cut off Brina's tail fin to see if he had legs. As Jared hacked at Brina with a knife, his own legs were being eaten by sand creatures. Ben was up another tree, this one surrounded by water. The water was rising and Ben was yelling at Charla to help him before it was too late. Over and over again Ben shouted, "I can't swim. I can't swim. Help! Charla help!"

"I can't help," Charla said in her dream. "I don't want to be a tree ape like Jared."

Charla woke and opened her eyes. She was glad to be awake and no longer dreaming. Light filtered through the trees. The interesting pattern of the night before still hung above her, but the pattern was no longer beautiful. In three places, birds struggled to break free.

"Chalk one up for being of the sea, and not of the air," Charla thought.

She lay back down and closed her eyes, reluctant to leave the water. Then Charla sat bolt upright. She was awake, but the voice of her dream continued. Ben was shouting, "Help! Charla! Help!"

Charla looked to where she had last seen Ben the night before. She saw a large black creature with eight legs standing over him. There was no sign of Jared. Charla transformed, stood up, and took her spear in one hand and her knife in the other. She left the safety of the water and silently crept forward. The creature never saw Charla coming as it continued to wrap Ben in a thread that it spun from its body. His legs were completely encased. His arms were held tight to his side. Ben struggled, but the thread held him secure. Only his head and shoulders were completely free.

Charla ran at the creature and buried her spear into its soft back. It reared up and fell backwards, driving the spear deeper into its body. Charla knelt beside Ben and began to cut the threads that held him secure. The creature rolled over and got to its feet. It ran towards Charla. She held her knife in front of her and when the creature came close enough, she lunged at it before dancing quickly away. Charla's knife sliced across one of the eight legs. The spider backed up and ran up a tree, the spear still buried in its back. It was over nine feet up when the spear snagged on a branch, causing the spider to lose its grip and fall back to the ground driving the spear right through its body. Its legs twitched violently in the air and then it lay still.

Charla cut the remaining threads away from Ben and helped him stand. They briefly stood there with their arms around one another for support.

"Jared…is up there," Ben said.

Charla followed his finger and saw a man-sized shape wrapped in sticky thread hanging upside-down from a branch high above their heads.

CHAPTER THIRTEEN

SPIDER'S NEST

Ben kicked off his shoes. There were no branches close to the ground for Ben to get hold of, but he imagined himself with suction cups and they appeared. He climbed the trunk of the tree until he reached the branch Jared was on. He took the knife Lea Waterborn had given him from its sheath and held it between his teeth. He threw one leg over each side of the branch and slid along it until he reached Jared.

At this point Ben paused. If he simply cut the two threads that secured Jared to the tree, Jared might well be hurt in the fall to the ground. The last thing Jared or any of them needed was a broken leg. He cut one thread and swayed on the branch as he struggled to hold part of Jared's weight. He put the knife in his mouth, suctioned himself to the branch with one hand and with the other wrapped the cut thread around his waist. The sticky thread stuck to itself and to him. Next, Ben cut the remaining thread that held Jared to the branch. He held his breath as he waited to see if a single thread would hold the weight of the Lushakan. The thread did not break, but Ben slipped off the branch when Jared's full weight hung from his waist.

Ben and Jared swung back and forth. Only one of Ben's hands held the branch. The weight on Ben's shoulder joint was painful. Without suction cups on his hand it would be impossible to hold on. Ben struggled to get his other hand attached to the branch so that he would stop swinging. He caught the branch with the suction cups of his three longest fingers and slowly inched his hand upwards until he had a good hold on the branch. Once he was secure Ben began the climb down.

When Jared was lowered to the ground, Charla took out her knife and carefully cut the web away from his head. Jared's face was pale. He did not appear to be breathing. As Charla continued to cut the spider web, Ben pinched Jared's nose and breathed air into his lungs.

When Ben sat back, Charla gently slapped Jared's face, "Come on, tree ape, wake up. I saved your life again, and I want to hear you say 'Charla's the best there is.'"

Jared's eyes fluttered and he moaned. Charla and Ben sat back and waited for Jared to recover. Ben and Charla's eyes scanned the trees and the surrounding forest anxiously as they waited.

"What happened?" Charla asked.

"It got us when we were asleep. I woke up to Jared's screams. The spider was wrapping him in a cocoon. I tried to get up but the spider had spun its web over me and I could not get free. I watched it take Jared up the tree and then come back down for me. I kept calling you, but you didn't hear."

Ben pointed out the large web with the struggling birds that hung across the river between two large trees. "It's a wonder we didn't see that web last night."

"I saw it, but there were no birds in it then and I didn't know what it was. Do you have such creatures on Earth? Is that why you know what they are and what a web is?"

"Yeah...sort of...but not anywhere near as big. The biggest one I've seen was about this big." Ben made a circle with his hands about five inches across.

"I could deal with something that size," said Charla.

"As long as you see it first," Ben said. "Some are poisonous. Their bite can be deadly."

"You were lucky I was here. Once again I saved your lives," said Charla smugly.

"Yes," Ben agreed unwillingly.

"You'd both be long dead without me," Charla boasted. "Wait until Lea Waterborn hears about this. She'll finally realize that I'm ready to be chosen."

Ben said nothing. The mermaid's arrogance was irritating, even if she had just saved his life once again. Ben changed the subject. "Charla, what were you doing following Brina and I?"

"All I ever get to do is watch for arrivals from other worlds. Other mer get chosen to go off world, but I never do. It is as if the Guardian does not know I exist. This time, it was Lea Waterborn's decision to make. I felt sure she would let me go. When I asked, Lea Waterborn said I wasn't ready. Wasn't ready!" Charla's voice became shrill. "I've been ready for a long time. I'm the best in my class at everything! All I need is a chance to prove myself. If only Lea Waterborn could see me now. She would know that I'm ready." Charla paused, and then said, "I was just going to follow you to the island and wait for you, but then Brina…"

Further conversation was halted by a loud groan from Jared. Charla took a seashell from her bag and scooped up some water. Ben helped Jared sit up. Charla held the shell to Jared's lips.

"Gone?" Jared asked, after he had recovered a bit.

"Yes," said Ben. "Charla killed it."

"…no…not again…to be free… must save…three times."

"Don't feel obligated. I didn't do it for you. I did it for Brina and for all the mer that will die if that crown is not retrieved. Your life is not worth anything to me."

Jared said nothing to Charla, but addressed Ben, "…thought you were hero…not mermaid…"

Ben said nothing, but took away his supporting arm from under Jared's shoulders. Jared's head thumped to the ground. He lay still a moment, then rolled over and pushed himself into a sitting position.

"How did you get me down?" Jared asked.

"I climbed the tree," Ben replied.

"You were high up, tree ape," Charla piped up, "which is where you would have stayed if it was up to me. That's where tree apes belong. I wouldn't climb a tree for you even if I could."

"How…?"

Ben called forth the suction cups and showed them to Jared.

"Wow… that and invisible…beginning to believe…you are from another world."

"Slow, isn't he?" Charla said. Jared gave Charla a dirty look, but said nothing. "I'll get some breakfast," Charla continued, "which will help the tree ape recover his strength. Not that I care. As far as I'm concerned, we should have left you up there for the spider."

Charla came back with three cleaned and filleted fish. When his meal was finished, Jared noticed Charla's spear sticking out of the spider. It was covered in inky goo. He stood, a bit shaky, and walked over to the spider. He pulled the spear out of its body. Then he cleaned the spear and gave it to Charla with a barely discernible 'thanks.' Jared's eyes stayed on his feet and he missed the fleeting smile on Charla's face, which had only a trace of smugness.

Ben meanwhile was skirting the edges of the clearing. After a careful search, Ben found two places where people had passed recently. He followed one of the two trails into the forest. Broken branches, grass trampled underfoot, scuff marks on the exposed rocky path all told him someone had passed by. Ben was so focused on the ground that he just about walked into a cave made from web. Scores of dinner-plate sized spiders hung from the ceiling and the walls. They stood piled on top of one another on the ground. Beyond them, Ben could see the massive body of a spider larger than the one that now lay dead in the clearing. The baby spiders had one goal in mind—him. Fortunately, they were not particularly brave. Ben picked a branch off the ground and swung it. The spiders closest to him jumped back and ran into the ones behind them. Ben swung the branch from side to side as he stepped back one foot at a time. The spiders kept coming towards him from their web cave. Ben turned and fled back towards the clearing.

Jared was sitting on the ground near the tree. Charla was sitting at the side of the stream with her mer tail in the water.

"Get up! Hurry! Spiders! Lots! Coming!" Ben yelled. Jared and Charla jumped up and met him in the clearing.

"What's wr...?" Jared began, but stopped as a spider leg rose up over Ben's shoulder. Jared turned Ben around, grabbed the spider, and threw it to the ground. Ben kicked the spider and sent it flying in the direction he had just come from. Its body fell in front of the spiders that were following it. The lead spiders stopped and began to eat their fallen comrade. The spiders just arriving walked over and around them. A flood of black covered the ground.

"I hate spiders," Ben said, his voice shaking as they all started to run towards the other path that led out of the clearing.

Ben looked over his shoulder and noticed that most of the baby spiders had stopped at the body of the spider Charla had killed. A few still trailed behind them. The three ran as fast and far as they could, which was not all that fast or far. Jared was still weak and Charla was having trouble running. Legs did not come naturally for her. She had mastered them at school, where she walked on level ground under her tutor's watchful eye. She was one of the best in her class, but she'd never run over rough ground before. Fear made it hard for her to concentrate on keeping legs. However, with much concentration Charla managed to keep her legs and not revert back to what was natural. When they stopped running there were only a few baby spiders nearby which were quickly killed.

CHAPTER FOURTEEN

OMNIVORES & CARNIVORES

The forest floor was covered with ferns, small bushes, and a lush variety of plant life. Trees towered overhead and blocked out most of the light. Logs had fallen across the path. The companions climbed over or ducked under many fallen trees. It was slow moving. Moss covered the fallen logs and went up the trunks of the living trees. Black and yellow slugs left a trail of slime behind themselves. The occasional bird flew from branch to branch and squirrels chattered in the trees.

They had been walking for over two hours when Ben came to an abrupt stop. Jared came to a stop behind Ben. Charla, who had been walking close behind Jared, ran into him.

"Fish breath, don't those fake legs of yours know how to stop?" Jared snorted.

Charla shoved Jared aside and stepped beside Ben, who had dropped down to his knees.

"What is it?" Charla asked.

"An animal, a large animal, maybe more than one," Ben answered. "They came out of the trees there." Ben pointed to a place where Charla and Jared could see something big had bent down the grass and broken low-hanging branches. Ben stood up and walked further along the trail before stopping again. A number of flies crawling on a brown pile flew up into the air and swarmed him. Ben slapped at them as he hunched down over the evil smelling animal excrement, or in other words pile of poop. He took a stick and began to stir the pile so that he could see what was in it. An unpleasant odor filled the air.

"Yuck," Charla exclaimed. "Leave it alone."

Jared grunted in agreement. "There is no gold crown in there."

Ben ignored them and continued to stir and examine the large pile of feces. Then he sat back with a worried look on his face.

"What is it? What did you find?" Jared asked.

Ben replied, "They are omnivores."

"What does that mean?" Charla asked.

"They eat both plants and other animals. We could look like a food group." Ben said flatly, not looking at Jared.

Jared spun around and looked at the trail they had been following. "Are you sure we've been following the trail left by my brother?"

"I don't know if it's your brother, but from what I've seen, humans passed by on this trail sometime recently," Ben replied.

"Do you think these creatures followed them?"

"I don't know."

"Should we leave the trail?" Charla asked.

"No," Ben said. "Those animals could be anywhere now; for all we know they could be following us."

"Then we should keep going," Jared said. "If my brother did pass by here we might find him up ahead roasting some omnivores for us."

"I hope so," Ben replied.

The three companions walked in silence, wondering what this new danger might look like. Occasionally, one of them turned and looked behind them. Once in a while they were forced off the trail to avoid a web that hung across it, but they always returned to it and continued the gradual climb to the top of the island's one mountain.

Ben broke the silence. "Good thing those spiders are cannibals or the island would be crawling with them."

"The same could be said for those spider crabs," Jared said.

Charla lagged further and further behind. Her inexperience with legs made walking hard and it was also the first time she had been in a forest. There were sights and sounds that she had never seen or heard in her life. She came to a complete stop to watch a group of large multi-colored butterflies flutter about a bush that was covered in flowers. Their wings shimmered when the light struck them. The flowers were beautiful to look at and smelled very pleasant. Charla was awe-stuck by this glimpse of unexpected beauty. She bent down to smell a particularly beautiful flower. When she looked up, Jared and Ben were out of sight. They had gone around a bend in the path. Charla hurried to catch up. When she caught sight of them, Charla stopped and called out, "Ben...ah." Ben and Jared turned just in time to see a spider drop down in front of Charla.

"I'll be right with you," Charla shouted, "just as soon as I kill myself another spider."

The spider ran at Charla on its eight legs. Charla kept her eye on the spider as she reached over her shoulder for her spear. A spider's leg came from behind and wrapped itself around her arm. Charla screamed and dropped the spear.

Jared and Ben ran back through the forest. Charla lay on the ground between two spiders, which were ready to do battle with each other to decide which one would have Charla for lunch. Charla lay on the ground like a fish out of water. A fish tail had replaced her legs. Terror tends to do that to the mer.

"Jared," Charla called, "if you want to get rid of one of your obligations this might be a good time to do it. Throw me my spear."

Jared may well have done so, but one of the spiders moved so that it stood directly over it.

Jared had his spear in one hand and a knife in the other, as did Ben. Jared attacked the closest spider, while Ben ran around and attacked the second one. Jared hacked at the legs with his knife, while keeping the spider's head away with his spear. He cut off one leg and damaged a second. The spider came at him on its remaining legs, hardly hampered by the loss.

Meanwhile, Ben plunged his spear into the second spider as he had seen Charla do. This one did not fall backwards. It turned with the spear in its back and ran at him. Ben ran straight towards a tree and up the trunk with his octopus hands. The spider ran up the tree after him. Ben wished himself invisible and he was. The spider stopped, looked around and came cautiously up the trunk of the tree. Ben sat on a branch and slid along it. The spider continued on past where Ben sat. Ben took off his shoes and hung them around his neck so that he would have the extra grip from the suction cups on his feet. He stood on the branch and was just about to return to the ground when the spider came down on a single thread. It passed his branch and was heading towards Charla, who stood with her hands on her hips watching Jared battle the spider that still stood over her spear. She was oblivious to the one dropping down on her from above.

Ben didn't stop to think about it. As the spider went past him, he dropped on top of it, and drove the spear that was in its back further down into the spider's body. The spider and Ben fell towards the ground. Ben held onto the spider with the suction cups on the bottom of his feet as they spun downwards. He continued to drive the spear further into the spider's body. The spider came to an abrupt halt and hung limply in the air. Ben pulled his spear out of the dead spider, and looked down.

Charla had a stick in her hand. With it she was poking the remaining spider from the side. It ignored her and continued its attack on Jared. Jared had a raw wound across his arm, where the barbs on the underside of the spider's legs had taken off skin. Ben launched himself into the air, hoping to land on the spider, and drive his spear into its back. Instead of landing on a soft spider he fell on the hard ground. The spider had moved forward just as he jumped. Ben lay on the ground, the breath knocked out of him. He rolled over and discovered that he was on the ground underneath the spider's belly.

He stood up and drove the spear into the spider from below. From the spider's wound gushed thick black blood, which splashed over Ben's head and down his body. The spider crumpled on top of him.

"Yuck! Get this thing off me, PLEASE!" Ben's muffled voice said from underneath the spider.

Jared and Charla grabbed the spider and rolled it over. Ben used Charla's spear to push himself up off the ground. When Charla grabbed her spear, Ben fell over.

"I asked you to give me this, not use it as a cane," Charla stated emphatically.

"A thank you would be nice. Let me show you how it's done. Thank you for saving my worthless, sorry life," Jared said, mimicking Charla's voice. "I'm sorry to be such a pain in the ass. I am forever in your debt, O most noble ones."

Charla ignored Jared. "Let me see either of you handle two spiders at once. I could have managed one without any help."

"From now on we stay close together," Ben stated firmly, ignoring the verbal exchange.

The three companions resumed walking. Charla kept quiet as the boys went over every detail of their battle with the spiders, clearly excited with their victory and the fact that they had finally turned the tables, and been the ones to save Charla's life.

Charla ended their conversation when she said, "Thank you, Jared, for saving my life. Please consider your obligation cancelled," Charla paused and then continued, "After all, a mer life is worth the life of at least three tree apes."

"That's not the way I see it," Jared said. "In fact, if you look at it that way, I would have to save your life a dozen more times before my obligation is paid in full."

The path brought them to a clearing. Before them was a waterfall that came down the side of a sheer high cliff into a pond below. Charla ran towards the pond and dove in. She quickly disappeared from sight. Ben and Jared walked a bit further on and drank from the waterfall.

Charla surfaced. Her tail slapped the water. The splash soaked Jared. Charla laughed before disappearing under the water again. When Charla reappeared, her face had lost some of the strained look it had taken on during their walk through the forest.

Ben touched Jared's wet arm. "Perhaps we can rest here for a little while before we continue on," he said.

Jared quickly agreed. The battle with the spider had taken its toll and he was tired.

"What's up?" Charla said as she surfaced in front of Ben and Jared.

"A rest," Jared replied.

Relief passed over Charla's face. "Well, if you two are tired then I think it wise that we rest."

Charla tossed two fish at Jared and Ben and then disappeared back into the water.

Ben took off his shoes, dropped his pack and walked into the pond fully clothed. When the water was waist deep, he dipped himself into the water several times to rid his hair and clothing of the spider guts that still clung to him. Jared had the fish filleted when Ben returned. This time he never stopped to think about the fact that he was eating raw fish; in fact, he was rather looking forward to it.

All the rest Charla needed was to be in her mer form, so she explored the pond and the waterfall. After Ben finished eating he walked along the stream where the water got shallower. Where the ground was soft he found two sets of human footprints. Overtop them were the footprints left by some very large animals. It was the same footprints that Ben had seen in the forest. Each animal foot had six toes with long sharp claws. Ben crossed over to the other side of the stream and searched for the place where the humans came out of the water. He did not find it. He came back over to the side where Jared lay sleeping and continued the search. He found no human footprints leaving the water at all. Ben did find the footprints of several large six toed animals coming to the water and leaving it on both sides of the pond.

"It's time for us to go," Ben said when Charla returned. I'll wake Jared up."

"If you must," Charla said, with a look of distaste on her face.

Ben was crouching beside Jared to shake him awake when a treg screamed overhead. Jared was instantly awake and they both scrambled underneath some low-hanging branches. Charla pulled herself along the bottom of the stream towards deeper water. The treg had seen Charla. It dove towards her. The treg was almost on top of Charla when she reached water that was deep enough to hide in. Jared and Ben held their breath and watched as the treg missed his prey. It screeched, rose into the air, and circled overhead.

CHAPTER FIFTEEN

THE UGLIES COMETH

The three companions sat on the ground under the thick branches of a tree. They looked anxiously at the sky as they discussed their options.

"Did you see any sign that Gill was here?" asked Jared.

"I don't know if it was your brother, but there were two humans here," Ben said.

"One of them died on the beach," Jared said and then paused. "I know that one set of the footprints here belongs to my brother. Gill's the best there is."

"Which way did they go?" Charla asked.

"I don't know," Ben said, unsure of whether to tell Jared about the vanishing footprints. "I lost their trail, but there is a path on the other side that runs alongside the cliff into the forest. It might take us to the top." Ben pointed to the top of the cliff.

"The trees should hide us from the tregs once we get across the river. But we will need to move quickly." Jared said.

The three companions crossed to the other side of the stream and walked along the bank towards the trail that ran alongside the cliff. There were many obvious signs that the six-toed creatures came often to the pool in front of the waterfall. There were footprints everywhere that came out of the forest to the pool and then led back into the forest.

"I think we should—" Ben began. His sentence was cut off by the bellow of an animal in the forest behind them. Something was coming along the trail they had walked that morning.

Emerging from the forest were two large creatures that looked like something out of earth's prehistoric past. They were large, hairless gray animals. Each had a tail tipped with two spikes. They were about the size of an elephant, but had an alligator shaped jaw from which several large teeth protruded. The only things small about them were their eyes, which is perhaps why they failed to see the three companions.

The two creatures nosed the place where Jared had fallen asleep. They clawed at the ground. Rocks, grass, and dirt flew through the air until there was a small mound behind each of them. When they found nothing one of them gave a mournful bellow. The bellow was answered by one in the forest in front of the companions, on the same side of the river they were now on. Something in the forest began to crash through the trees towards them. The ones across the stream looked up and saw the three companions for the first time.

"They are coming from both sides," Ben said, his voice hoarse. He looked around, desperate for some escape route. "Maybe we can climb the cliff."

The three took a few quick steps towards it. It was very sheer, with few handholds. It would be no problem for Ben with his octopus ability, and perhaps he could help one other person up, but the one left on the ground would certainly be dead.

Charla looked from the creatures to the cliff and lost her balance, because her legs began their transformation back into a fish tail. Ben did not see her dilemma. His eyes were on the cliff he was anxious to climb. Jared, however, saw what was happening to Charla.

"My turn," Jared said, as he grabbed Charla around the waist, threw her over his shoulder and sprinted towards the pond. Jared jumped into the water carrying Charla and the two of them disappeared momentarily from sight.

When they surfaced, Charla called, "Come this way Ben. You'll be safe under the waterfall."

Ben stood undecided. He looked at the water, the cliff, and the animals. He considered leaving Charla and Jared to take their chances in the water while he climbed the cliff. He could climb the cliff easily, but could he really leave them? He would be safe, but Jared and Charla might not be. The creatures might be good swimmers. Would they really find safety in the water?

"Come on Ben," Jared called.

Ben's feet were moving towards the water even as his mind was telling him that the best escape for him was to climb the cliff. When he reached the edge of the water, he stopped. He stepped back and turned towards the cliff, just as a fourth creature came from the trail they had planned to take. It was closer to the cliff than Ben. It was no longer possible to escape that way even if he wanted to. Ben stepped back and then took a running jump into the water. He sank, but two hands reached down and pulled him to the surface.

"Now what?" he gasped, his feet kicking frantically.

"The waterfall," said Charla. We'll be safe from the uglies behind it."

"Uglies?" Jared asked.

"Do you have a better name for them?" Charla said and moved behind Ben and slipped her arms around his chest. "Relax," she said. "I will take you to the waterfall."

Relaxing is not something Ben was capable of doing in water, but he slowed his frantic kicking and let Charla drag him towards the waterfall. From his position Ben saw two of the creatures enter the water where he had just been standing. When the waterfall hit his face, Ben began to struggle, but Charla held him tight. From the backside of the waterfall the three turned and looked through the water to see that the four large creatures had all entered the water and were swimming towards them.

"What are we going to do?" Jared asked. "It looks like they are good swimmers.

"There's a cave," Charla replied.

"Where?" Ben asked, scanning the rock wall behind the waterfall.

"Underwater," Charla replied.

"Wait a minute," Jared said. "Ben and I don't do underwater. We don't come equipped with gills."

Ben struggled in Charla's arms, a horrified look on his wet face. Charla tightened her grip on Ben.

"You can do what you like tree ape, but if you stay here I predict an untimely end to your miserable life. Ben and I are leaving here now. If you know what's good for you, you will follow me. There is an underwater passageway that comes out in a cave where you will be able to breathe air."

Ben continued to struggle.

"Let me go," he hollered.

"Breathe Ben," she commanded.

"No…wait…I," Ben began.

Charla ignored him. "Breathe," she commanded again.

Ben managed to fill his lungs just before Charla dragged him underwater. Charla dragged Ben down the rock wall behind the falls until they came to a narrow opening. Ben kicked his legs and did his best to move himself in the direction Charla was dragging him. Jared followed. As they entered the cave, Ben's sense of panic grew. Not only was he underwater, but he was underwater in the dark. Being underwater in the dark was the very dream that haunted Ben. Wild thoughts raced through his mind. But the real question was whether Charla knew how long a human being could stay underwater before needing to breathe.

In the darkness of the underwater cave it was impossible to tell whether they were going up or down, left or right. Ben and Jared were not able to see, but Charla, being mer was able to see her way in the almost total darkness. Ben was weak with fear and had come to the end of his ability to hold his breathe when they emerged into a small pond in the middle of a dark cave. Charla pushed Ben out of the water and up onto the rock and then watched anxiously for Jared to appear. On his hands and knees, Ben spit out water, gasping and coughing. He hardly heard Charla when she said, "I'll go look for the tree ape."

Charla disappeared into the water and Ben was alone in the dark cave.

Charla moved quickly through the underwater passage. She made her way back to the waterfall but did not see Jared. She popped her head out of the cave and saw that one of the uglies was behind the waterfall. She turned around and swam back along the passage, running her hands along the rock as she went. She came to a place where a passage led to the left, a passage she had missed earlier. It was here that she found Jared. He had breathed out the last of his air. Charla put her lips over Jared's. She breathed in through the gills behind her ears and breathed out through her mouth. Jared clutched at her arms, terrified that she would take her life-giving lips away. Charla maneuvered Jared out of the dead-end passage and dragged him to where she had left Ben.

Ben watched the pond anxiously. Relief flooded through Ben when he saw the water swirl and Jared's head appear. Charla held Jared while his strength returned. Then she supported him as he feebly climbed out of the water.

"In a little while I'll go see if the uglies are still at the waterfall," said Charla, her voice shaking slightly.

Ben lay back and closed his eyes. He was horrified at the thought of going through the dark underwater passage again. When he opened his eyes, he looked at the ceiling and could clearly see a narrow opening from which a dim light shone.

"That may not be necessary," Ben said as he sat up. "I may be able to climb through that crevice and look over the cliff."

Ben took off his sneakers and stood up. He banged his head against the top of the cave and promptly sat down again. When the pain subsided, Ben stood up more carefully and walked hunched over to the crevice, where he stood up without banging his head. He firmly attached his hands to the rock, and pulled himself up until he could attach the suction cups on his feet.

It was an easy climb, at least for someone with suction cups on his hands and feet. The crevice did not come straight down from the surface, but angled off to the right at a steep angle. Ben was about halfway up when he heard Charla sob.

"Lea Waterborn is right. I'm not ready. I can't maintain my transformation when I'm afraid. I should never have come," the mermaid said.

He could hear Jared voice murmur a response, but he did not catch the words.

When Ben reached the top, he was in a shallow cave that opened towards the forest. Ben walked out of the cave towards the stream that tumbled over the edge to become the waterfall they had seen from below. When he got close to the stream he dropped on his hands and knees and crawled until he could lay down with his head hanging over the edge of the cliff. He could see the pond below. One of the uglies was swimming back and forth in front of the waterfall. Another ugly was just leaving the water. Another one was on shore digging at the spot where the three companions had last stood. A fourth was looking up at him as he looked down at it. The creature's gaze unnerved Ben and he pushed himself back. As he did so, Ben dislodged a rock. It caught other loose rocks on the way down. Ben moved forward again to see what was happening.

The ugly came forward and sniffed the rock that Ben had knocked over the edge. It bellowed and charged towards the rock wall. Ben froze. His mind told him those things could not climb a sheer cliff, but he still held his breath in fear. He watched the ugly charge the cliff at full speed right where the rocks had come down. The ugly hit the rock wall hard and fell down. It thrashed about and then got back on its feet where it swayed back and forth.

"Dumb as nails," Ben muttered.

The other three came and stood beside the one that had rammed the cliff. They nosed all over the area where the ugly had charged, particularly the rock that Ben's hand had rested on. Then they looked up to the top of the cliff. Ben did not think they saw him for there was no bellow. Three of the uglies turned and lumbered off along the trail that the three companions had planned to take. The fourth ugly, still recovering from hitting solid rock followed at a slower and somewhat erratic pace.

Ben rolled over in time to see a treg swooping down on him. Its claws stretched out to pick him off the cliff. If Ben had waited three seconds more before rolling over it would have had him. Ben lay still on the ground with his invisibility turned on. He could not remember if birds had good hearing or a good sense of smell. If it was a good sense of smell then Ben should move quickly, but if it was an acute sense of hearing then he should lay still and try to keep his breathing slow and quiet. Ben could have reached out his hand and touched the bird, but he did not move a muscle. He lay still and looked at the treg. The treg peered around intently, cocking its bald red head first one way and then another, listening for a sound to tell it which way its prey had gone. Ben lay still and did not move. The treg was big. It was as tall as he was. The treg's beak was curved and sharp. It was the beak of a predator.

The treg must have heard a suspicious noise. It turned towards Ben and looked directly at him, cocking its head this way and that. Ben held his breath even when he saw something he never expected to see. The treg was wearing a collar.

The treg turned away, walked towards the cliff edge and jumped off as it stretched its wings. It caught the air currents and rose high up into the air. Its shadow passed over Ben and it flew back towards the center of the island, where it landed on a rock outcropping. It turned in Ben's direction and stood like a sentinel, watching for any movement on the mountain.

CHAPTER SIXTEEN

INVISIBLE BEN

The stream came from the center of the island. It came out of the heart of a volcanic cone. Over the years it had cut a deep, narrow ravine into the volcanic rock at the top of the mountain. Between the ravine and the waterfall was a rocky hillside on which only a few stunted trees grew. The distance between the ravine and the waterfall was approximately a quarter-mile. It was not far, but the tregs would see anything moving across the hillside.

Ben took out his knife and cut down four small leafy trees. He took them to the mouth of the cave and then went back down the crevice. When Ben returned to the underground cave he was surprised by what he saw. Charla and Jared were sitting by the pond. Jared's arm was around Charla and her head was resting on his shoulder. As soon as Ben hit the ground with a thud they moved apart.

There was an embarrassed silence. "Are the uglies still there?" Charla finally said.

"No. They've gone."

"Then we can leave," Charla said as she dropped into the dark water.

Ben shuddered and said, "Not that way. The crevice leads to the top of the waterfall. The uglies have taken the path we were going to take. They can't see well, but they have an acute sense of smell. They knew I was above them, and I think they are coming this way."

"We're no match for one ugly, let alone four," Jared said. "And Charla is…"

"Charla is what, tree ape?" the mermaid demanded.

"It is clear," Jared said, "that each hour we spend on land gets harder for you. How long will you be able to keep your transformation?"

"Worry about yourself. I can go on as long as I need to," Charla stated in a strong voice, then after a slight pause, she said quietly, "I hope."

"Neither of you need to come," Ben said. "You two can head back to sea. I'm the one the Guardian chose; there is no need for the two of you to risk your lives."

"I'm coming with you," said Jared. "My dream said that I would go to the top of the mountain. I need to get to Gill before it's too late."

"Charla could stay here till we come back," Ben said, "and if we don't come back in a day try to make her way back to the sea alone."

"Forget it," said Charla.

"I agree with Charla," Jared said.

"You do?" Charla said, clearly surprised. "Well at least we agree on something, tree…" Charla stopped speaking in mid-sentence. She then repeated herself, "At least we agree on something…Jared."

"None of us should stay behind. There is no guarantee we will be able to come back this way. It would be hard for any one of us to survive this island alone. We can give Charla whatever help she needs," Jared stated firmly.

"If you're determined, then we should go this way," Ben said, pointing to the crevice. "There are good handholds. It won't be too difficult for Jared, and Charla can make it with our help. But we should go now! The uglies are on their way."

Jared and Charla stood. Ben boosted Jared up. Once Jared had a good hold, Ben boosted Charla. Jared grabbed her hand and told her where to find a handhold for the other one. They began the climb up the crevice, with Jared reaching down to help Charla when he could, and Ben boosting her from below.

As they climbed Ben said, "I saw a treg up close, closer than I ever want to be again. It came from behind while I was looking over the cliff and just about got me before I became invisible. The treg was wearing a collar."

"A collar!" exclaimed Charla.

"Are you sure?" asked Jared.

"I'm very sure," Ben said.

"What does it mean?" Charla wondered.

"It means someone is controlling the tregs," Ben said.

"That makes sense," broke in Jared. "That's why they're taking things they've never been interested in before."

Soon they were all standing on the surface, under a large tree near the small cave, from where they could look across the bare hillside to the center of the island.

"Keep out of sight," Ben said quietly, as he pointed out the perched treg. "We've got to get to the ravine. It's too narrow for either the tregs or the uglies. We will be safe once we get there, if it's possible to be safe anywhere on this island."

"I hope you're right about that ravine not being wide enough," Jared said. "But the real problem is getting across the hill to the ravine."

"The tregs will see us. We will not get far with them standing watch," Charla said.

"I have an idea," Ben said as he picked up the small trees he had cut. He gave one each to Jared and Charla. "Hold a branch in front of you. I will turn on my invisibility and stand between you holding a tree branch behind each of you. The branches should hide you from the tregs. If we go slowly enough, the tregs may not notice that the trees are moving."

"It might work," Jared said, "as long as the uglies do not catch up to us."

With those words, Charla picked up one of the small trees and held it in front of her.

"Let's go," she ordered. "Let's go now."

There was no argument from either Ben or Jared. Jared picked up one of the bushy trees Ben had cut, while Ben took one in each hand. They walked along, doing their best to ensure that their bodies were not visible to the tregs sitting on rock outcroppings.

They left the shelter of the cave and began to take their first slow steps.

"One more thing," Ben said quietly, "tregs can hear really well. It might be wise not to talk from here to the ravine. And the uglies have a wonderful sense of smell, so no farting."

Jared chuckled quietly.

"Mer do not fart," Charla said indignantly.

They followed the creek because it was where they would blend in because the stubby trees were thickest. Charla and Jared walked close together so that the small trees they held would provide the maximum amount of screening. They took a step forward, paused, and then took another small step. A treg rose in the air and flew towards them. They stood perfectly still as it flew above them, banked, and returned to its roost. The three friends took even smaller steps and paused longer before they stepped again. The ground sloped uphill and there were places where they had to risk a bigger step so they could stand without risking a fall. The treg closest to the three companions seemed to know something was not right. It became more and more agitated. Occasionally it stretched its wings as if to take flight, only to settle down again as the three companions stopped moving. They slowly moved across the barren hillside.

More than a half hour had passed and they were just over half way to the ravine. Ben's arms were aching from the effort of holding the two small trees. He did not know how long he could continue to carry the weight. It would have been easier if he could move his arms, but he had to hold them steady so that the walking trees did not arouse suspicion. His plan was turning into a test of endurance. He was feeling sorry for himself when his eyes caught a movement to the west of them. It was two of the uglies. They were moving slowly towards the waterfall with their noses close to the ground. Occasionally one or the other would look up and scan the horizon, but they saw nothing that aroused their suspicion. Ben was trying to think of a way to let Jared and Charla know without speaking that the uglies had arrived. He did not want to risk attracting the tregs. One of the uglies snorted loudly and there was no need.

Charla and Jared began to walk a bit faster. A treg lifted off its perch and flew towards them. The three companions stood still and hoped that the treg would not see anything suspicious between the leaves of the four small trees that met just over their heads. The treg circled above them for a moment and then flew toward the uglies. A second treg to the west of them had taken to its wings and was flying toward the uglies. The two tregs harassed the uglies. They attacked their broad backs with their razor sharp beaks. The uglies bellowed and swung their spiked tails at the birds. They snapped their massive jaws shut whenever the birds got too close to their heads.

"Walk fast," Ben whispered. "Don't stop until I tell you!" The three companions made fast progress while the attention of the tregs and the uglies was focused on each other.

Ben kept his head turned and watched the battle. Unfortunately, it did not last long. Soon the three companions were standing still as the tregs flew back to their perches. The uglies continued their slow snuffling walk toward the waterfall. The three companions were now about three-quarters of the way across the hillside.

The uglies bellowed behind them. They had picked up their scent and turned towards the center of the mountain. Ben looked behind them and confirmed that the uglies were coming their way at a lumbering run. The tregs became agitated. They rose from their perches and flew over the three companions to once again attack the uglies. Two tregs from perches further away flew towards them from the east and the west. Ben looked over his shoulder and saw that the uglies were closing the gap in spite of being under attack by the tregs.

"Run," Ben whispered urgently. "Fast!"

The three companions threw aside the small leafy trees and sprinted toward the ravine. The uglies bellowed and picked up speed. Luckily for the three companions they were not the fastest of creatures. The two tregs continued to attack the uglies, while two other tregs, one from the West and another from the East flew toward the three companions. The tregs screeched and the uglies bellowed as the three companions ran as fast as they could.

Ben pulled ahead of the other two, and had almost reached the safety of the ravine when he noticed Charla and Jared were not running with him. He looked over his shoulder and saw that Charla's legs had turned into a tail fin, and Jared was trying to carry her on his back. Ben looked at the ravine. He was almost safe. If he kept running he would live. If he stopped and turned back he almost certainly would die. Ben paused for just a moment, unsure of what to do. Then he turned and ran back to Charla and Jared. Jared and Ben linked arms and picked Charla up.

The uglies lumbered heavily on. The sound grew louder with each passing moment. Ben could have sworn he felt their breath on his back every time they wheezed. The two tregs that had flown out to harass the uglies had not yet seen the three companions, which was lucky as these tregs were closer than the other two and fast enough to have caught them. If it was a choice between uglies or tregs, Ben felt they would be better off being carried away by tregs than torn limb-from-limb by the uglies.

Charla looked behind them as the two boys carried her towards the safety of the ravine.

"Run! Run faster! The uglies are catching up. They're right behind us!" she screamed.

Ben didn't need Charla to tell him that. He could smell their stinky breath and feel the movement of air on his sweat-soaked back.

"The tregs have seen us!" Charla shouted. The tregs that were harassing the uglies noticed for the first time that they had another quarry. They flew straight up into the air and looped around and flew over the backs of the uglies towards the three companions. With a bird closing in on either side and two coming from behind, and two uglies breathing down their necks, the two boys ran on, carrying Charla between them.

Charla and Jared screamed. A moment later Ben's feet left the ground. He and Jared were gripping each other's arm, and Charla was holding tightly to each one of them. A treg had Jared in its talons and was lifting all three companions into the air out of reach of the uglies. The three companions shot forward towards the ravine as the treg tried to gain altitude. It could have managed just one of them easily, but the three companions maintained their hold on one another and it was too much for the bird. It dropped them into the stream, just in front of the ravine entrance. The uglies charged onwards as Ben, Jared and Charla scrambled into the ravine. The uglies splashed through the water towards the ravine opening. It was too narrow for one ugly, let alone two. The uglies crashed into each other and the rock on either side of the ravine and fell down in a tangle of legs. The tregs attacked the uglies as they thrashed about on the ground. The uglies roared their disappointment and their rage at being attacked by the birds. The three companions watched from the safety of the ravine as the uglies untangled themselves, awkwardly stood up, and ran back towards the waterfall. The tregs harassed them all the way across the hillside.

Jared and Ben pulled themselves onto a ledge that ran alongside the stream. They lay on the ledge, chests heaving, mouths open, gulping air. Charla lay in the middle of the stream, her eyes closed, and her mermaid's tail moving just enough to keep from getting carried downstream and out of the ravine into the open.

Charla swam over to the ledge and pulled herself up, still in her mermaid form.

"Are you guys okay?" she asked.

Charla pulled Jared's shirt aside to reveal two punctures in his chest that were seeping blood. Jared cried out in pain as the cloth of his shirt pulled away from the wounds on his shoulder. Charla looked at his other shoulder and saw two more spots of blood. She opened her backpack and took out a jar of healing ointment. Very gently Charla smeared ointment on Jared's wounded shoulders.

"We were lucky," Jared said through clenched teeth. "If the treg hadn't picked us up, the uglies would have had us."

Charla finished putting on the cream, but kept her hand on Jared's shoulder.

It was growing dark as the three companions moved further up the ravine until they found a suitable place to spend the night.

CHAPTER SEVENTEEN

TREGS TO THE RESCUE

Morning found the three friends despondent and afraid of what the day would bring. Charla and Ben opened their backpacks and shared their food with Jared. They ate in silence, each one lost in their own thoughts.

"I'm sorry!" Charla said finally, her eyes closed tightly to keep tears from leaking out.

"What for?" Jared asked with a look of concern on his tired face.

"I just about got you both killed. When I'm frightened I can't seem to keep my transformation. What was easy before is hard now."

"You're getting tired. We all are. I'm finding it more difficult to keep going and legs are natural for me. And staying invisible is getting harder the more tired I get. So it's no wonder that you are having a hard time," Ben said.

"But you haven't even begun to train yet. I've been training for two years. I should be able to do better. If something like that happens again, just leave me behind. I don't want to be the cause of your death—either one of you," Charla's tears flowed freely now.

Jared laid his hand gently on Charla's tail. Charla's eyes met Jared's and he smiled reassuringly. "What we've faced would frighten anyone."

"For sure," Ben said. "This place should be called Death Island, rather than Spenser Island."

"But...I must be able to hold a transformation if I'm ever going to be chosen to go off world. The Watcher was right. I'm not ready. Perhaps I never will be..."

"We wouldn't have made it this far without you. You saved both our lives more than once," Jared broke in.

"Jared's right," Ben said, his eyes closed. "We have a saying on our world, a true one I think; 'Only fools are never afraid.' Besides," Ben added, "I've been chosen, and I've been more afraid than either of you. If it were up to me, we'd have turned back a long time ago."

"Well, that's true," Charla said. "I've never met anyone who is afraid of water before."

"I've had dreams ever since I was little," Ben said. "I have dreams where I drop out of the sky into deep water. I can't breathe and it's dark. I call out for my mother, but she does not come. Everything goes dark. I float near death."

"Is it a memory?" Jared asked.

"I've wondered that myself," Ben replied. "Whatever it is, the Guardian made a mistake in choosing me. The only reason I've made it this far is that the two of you are with me. You two are the ones I would choose if I was doing the choosing."

"Us two?" Jared asked.

"Yes, you two!"

"How does one get to be chosen?" Jared asked.

"I don't know. All I know is that my dad is a Chosen and so was my grandmother. I think my mom was a Chosen as well. My dad and grandmother both went to the same school I go to, but I don't know about my mom. She must have, I guess. My dad is off somewhere doing the Guardian's work. He's been away for eight months. He told me that he would be gone just a few weeks. I'm afraid something happened to him and I'll never see him again. I didn't know what my dad did or anything about the six worlds until I went to Miss

Templeton's office three days ago. If someone had told me about the Guardian, Watchers, Chosen and portals to other worlds, I would have thought they were nuts."

"At Fairwaters, all the students know about the purpose of the school, but not all are chosen to go off world," Charla said. "Jared, you would be a Chosen if humans still trained at Fairwaters."

"There used to be humans?" Jared asked.

"Yes, humans and mer trained together, although some say that humans were never more than the servants of the Chosen."

"I don't understand," Ben said. "You accept that humans are chosen from other worlds, why not this world?"

"We...many of us...but not all...believe the humans on Lushaka are inferior to the humans from other worlds. We...some anyway believe that the humans of Lushaka would never be chosen no matter what world they lived on because they are an inferior breed of human."

"Is that what you think?" Jared asked.

"I used to think that way," Charla said.

"What happened?" Jared asked.

"I met you, tree ape, and knowing you changed my mind."

"No, I meant what happened to cause humans to stop training at Fairwaters?"

"There was a war between humans and mer. The students at Fairwaters got drawn into the conflict. All the humans and over half the mer were expelled. There haven't been any humans since."

"We've stories of that war. We have stories of people who betrayed us because they were not really human, but mer with the ability to look human. Changelings, we call them. Because of the changelings many of my people died. We are taught that every changeling must die. We are taught that if we know someone is a changeling and allow that person to live, then we are disloyal to our people and a disgrace to our ancestors. I never knew that a changeling could be someone...I...I..." Jared's voice trailed off.

"Jared, when I get back to Fairwaters, I will tell the Watcher about you. I will tell everyone who will listen that I've met a Lushakan human who is intelligent, has true courage, and can be trusted. I will tell everyone who will listen that you are worthy of being a student at Fairwaters."

Jared looked at Charla and then looked upstream in the direction they needed to go, speculation clearly written on his face. "We should go," he said finally and got to his feet.

Ben and Jared walked beside the stream when they could. In places where the gravel ledge disappeared, they took to the water. Charla stayed in the water and swam where she could. Where the water was shallow, she slid over the rocks as she pulled herself along with her hands to avoid changing from her mer form. When they hit the first waterfall, Charla transformed so that she could use her legs to climb to the next level. They had gone over six small waterfalls when they found themselves in a place where the ravine opened up and a pool had formed below yet another waterfall. Charla dove into the deep pool in the center of the ravine, while Jared and Ben walked around the outside of the pool towards the next waterfall.

The ravine was wider at this point. Up until they point they had walked in the shadow of the ravine wall, but now the sun shone down on the path the boys walked. Jared and Ben's shadows were cast on the wall beside them. Their shadows disappeared for a moment as the boys passed a dark crevice in the wall. Shortly thereafter, their shadows were joined by another shadow that towered above them. Jared heard a scraping sound and turned around. He squeaked out the word 'run', then sprinted ahead, dragging Ben with him. Ben looked over his shoulder and saw the snake, then put on his brakes. Ben dragged Jared, who was not willing to release his grip on his friend, to a stop.

"Don't be afraid," Ben said. "It's just an illusion. I've run into this before."

Ben stepped in front of Jared and took two steps back towards the snake. The snake reared back and spat. The spit hit the rock not far from Ben's feet. Some of it splashed on Ben's pant leg. He looked down in astonishment at the hole that appeared in his pants. Then he whispered hoarsely, "This one is real."

They were about to run when Charla surfaced close to the snake. She took in the situation, and like Ben thought the snake was an illusion.

"Impressive," Charla said. She reached out and touched the coiled body of the snake. Shock registered on Charla's face when her hand did not go right through the body of the snake. She finned backwards as the snake's head turned from the boys and chased her across the pond.

"Charla!" Jared screamed. "Go deep and hide."

Charla looked inclined to argue, but the snake was closing in rapidly. She disappeared underwater and sped down to the depths of the pond. The snake was not deterred. It followed her down. Charla hid behind a leafy plant. The snake stuck out its tongue, looking for her scent. Its head swiveled around looking for any sign of movement. It was inches away from Charla when its body convulsed. On the surface Jared had driven his spear into the tail end of the snake. Ben and Jared ran towards the next waterfall while the snake rapidly recoiled itself back on land.

As Jared ran his feet were lifted off the ground. It was not the snake who had him, but a treg. Here, the ravine was wide enough for a treg to fly into, and one had. When Jared was carried away the snake turned its full attention onto Ben. Ben cloaked himself in invisibility. The snake stopped when Ben disappeared, but then began to test the air with its tongue. It tested the air, and moved ever closer to Ben. Ben found he had to strain to hold onto his invisibility. Like Charla, he was tired and he was afraid. It was hard to hold his transformation. Ben walked backwards to the next waterfall keeping his eye on the snake. The snake kept testing the air with its tongue as it followed his movements. Then the snake's great head shot out over the water and around behind him. Ben was trapped between the main part of the snake and its head. The only way to freedom was up. Fortunately Ben could call forth the suction cups on his hands and feet. He began to climb. The snake tested the air with its tongue. It followed the invisible Ben as he climbed upwards.

Ben had a problem. He did not have the energy to maintain both invisibility and octopus hands. To lose his octopus hands would be to fall, so Ben became visible. He then climbed as fast as he could. His plan was to get to the top, run along it and then come down further along the ravine and meet up with Charla. But the snake was faster than he was. It was almost a relief when Ben felt sharp claws grab his shoulders. Ben released his hold on the rock so the treg could carry him away. He did not know what would happen to him as the prey of a treg, but he felt sure the snake planned to make an immediate meal of him. He could picture the snake opening its hinged mouth to swallow him whole. He likely would not be dead when the digestive juices began their work. The treg might also make a meal out of him, but that fate was not as immediate as the one the snake had in mind.

As Ben was being carried away he looked down and saw that Charla had transformed into her human legs and was climbing the next waterfall. He breathed a sigh of relief that she was getting away from the snake.

The treg carried Ben out of the bowl and on up to the top of the mountain. Once it reached the summit, it banked and began to drop towards the ground. The treg's wings beat the air to stop its descent and it released its hold on Ben. Ben looked down and felt a momentary relief that there was no water under his feet. He fell about eight feet onto very solid rock and for the first time Ben appreciated the benefits of falling into water.

CHAPTER EIGHTEEN

IN A CAGE

Ben's fall jarred his bones and rattled his teeth. He fell painfully on his knees. Ben sat back and looked around. He was in metal cage with no roof. Each wall of the cage was topped with wicked-looking circles of barbed wire. The barbed wire would cut Ben to sheds should he try to climb over. The cage had a distinctive feature that made escape difficult. The cage had no door.

The cage was off to one side in a circular valley surrounded by high cliffs. Escape from the inside of the volcanic cone would be almost impossible for anyone without suction cups on their hands and feet. The sheer rock walls made the valley a natural prison with no way out for those who could not fly. The floor of the valley was strewn with rocks and bones. Some of the bones were sun-bleached and dry. Other bones looked as if the flesh had recently been stripped from them. They were blood red. There was a large rock beside a natural spring that bubbled up from the valley floor. The water from the spring ran just on the other side of the cage so the prisoners had access to it. The water went underground and disappeared through a hole in the valley floor just before it reached the side of the cliff. This was the source of the stream the three friends had followed. Not far away was a pile of things that the tregs had collected. Ben's gym bag sat near the top. Somewhere in that pile would be the crown they had come to retrieve.

Off to the left there was a wooden structure. A roof supported by tall posts kept rain off a raised platform. The roof protected at least forty small monitors. Under each monitor was an identical set of buttons and switches. Nearby was a metal box that looked like a large coffin standing on end. The box, unlike the cage, had a door that was held shut with a metal bar. There was a small window at the top or the door.

A small creature covered with hair stood in front of the monitors. The creature's face and fingers were the only parts of it that were hairless. It had a protruding jaw and thick lips. The creature stood watching the screens and occasionally pushed a button or pulled a switch.

Ben looked up to the tops of the cliffs and saw two tregs sitting on nests. There were other nests, but they were empty.

"Ben! Ben!" A weak voice called his name. Brina was sitting against the fence near one corner of the cage. His tail was stretched out in front of him. It was dry and dull looking. His voice was raspy and weak. He did not look at all well. Ben got up and walked somewhat shakily over to Brina and sat down beside him.

"You're here," Brina whispered hoarsely.

"Yes," Ben replied.

"Charla?" Brina croaked out.

"She was alive a few minutes ago."

"Then … still hope."

"You knew she was following us?"

"I knew."

Ben took off his backpack and took out the seashell he carried. He ran over to the stream and put his arm through the wire of the cage and scooped up some water. He gave Brina the water to drink. Then he took off his shirt, ran back and dipped it in the water and spread it over Brina's dry tail fin.

"He knew…insisted…transform…they saw," Brina pointed to where Jared stood in excited conversation with two young men. One looked much like Jared and he was clearly unhappy.

"Is it the humans who are treating you badly? Ben asked confused.

"They are not giving me any food. They are also trying to keep me from water," Brina said. "But the old man has helped me."

An old man who was also a captive in the cage was sat on the ground not far from Brina. While they watched he grabbed the fence and dragged himself up from the ground. He walked unsteadily towards Ben and Brina.

"So the old man insisted you transform?" Ben asked, still confused.

"Not the old man, the dragon," Brina said and pointed outside of the cage.

The only creature Ben could see outside the cage was the ape-man. And he couldn't believe that he had heard Brina right. So he asked again, "Who knew you were mer?"

"The dragon."

"Dragon?"

For an answer Brina pointed to the center of the small valley to what Ben took to be a large rock. But as he looked closer he could discern features he had overlooked: a ridge along the spine, a tail wrapped around the body.

"One good thing…dragon does not like mer…I'm emergency rations…sorry my friend…you he likes." Brina's voice was stronger, but he was still struggling. "Dragon will eat…old man…before me."

"Oh, I'm far too stringy for the dragon to eat; besides Zork would rather keep me alive to torment. The name is Morton," The old man said.

Loud voices turned Ben's attention away from the old man to the other occupants of the cage.

"You promised you wouldn't follow me," the young man Ben understood to be Gill said.

"I promised not to follow you on my own. I wasn't on my own," Jared replied.

"You should not have come," Gill insisted.

"I knew you were in trouble. I dreamed that you needed me."

"A lot of good it will do. Now you'll rot in this cage with the rest of us, if you live long enough," Gill said as he stared towards Ben and Brina frowning.

The old man spoke loudly to the three Lushakans at the far end of the cage, "You'll wake the dragon if you keep that up." The dragon snorted, and changed position. Everyone, including Ben, froze. Ben walked over to where Jared stood with his brother.

"Ben, this is my brother Gill and his friend, Arno. Drenid died on the beach. There is no word of what happened to the other three."

"I'm sorry," Ben said.

"I understand that Jared would be dead if it was not for you," Gill said to Ben.

"I saved his life, he saved mine, and Charla saved us both more than once," Ben replied.

"Charla? Who's Charla?" Gill asked.

"Charla is a mermaid," Ben replied.

"What were you doing with a mer?" Gill demanded of Jared.

"She was helping us rescue you and find that stupid crown," Jared said heatedly.

"Is she a changeling?" Gill asked between clenched teeth.

"What do you know about the dragon?" Ben said to change the subject.

"The dragon wakes up sometime around sundown. If the tregs do not bring something else to eat, one of us will die." Ben looked at the sky. It was midday. There were still several hours until sundown.

"And how do you know this? Have you seen it?" Ben asked.

"The dragon told us," said Arno.

"It speaks?" Ben asked.

"Yeah! It speaks. It never gets tired of hearing the sound of its own voice."

"Perhaps it lies."

"No, the old man has seen it eat both human and mer. Look for yourself." Arno pointed to a ledge part way up the cliff. A few dozen human or mer skulls sat on the ledge and were staring vacantly down at them. Ben stared at the skulls as he walked towards the stream to get more water for Brina. He was handing the shell filled with water to Brina when it was knocked out of his hand.

"We do not give water to that thing," Gill's voice growled. "It's a changeling, a changeling who should be dead by now."

Gill gave the old man a menacing look. The old man moved away from them and sat down by himself.

"That thing is Brina and he's my friend."

Gill pushed Ben. "What kind of scum names a changeling as a friend? Unless you're a changeling too?"

A loud snort from the dragon reminded the cage occupants that they did not want to wake it.

"I'm going to get Brina some water now. If you try to stop me, there will be a lot of noise, which all of us will regret, but one of you will regret it more than I will."

"Suit yourself. You choose your friends and I'll choose mine," Gill said as he walked away from Ben to the other end of the cage.

Jared walked with Ben to the stream and whispered, "I'm sorry. He doesn't understand. But he's got a good heart and he'll come around. I know he will." Jared then walked away from Ben to join his brother.

Ben got Brina some more water to drink. He took his shirt off Brina's tail and took it to the stream. He placed it in the stream and then carried the dripping wet shirt to place it once more across Brina's tail fin. Ben sat down beside Brina who did not have the energy to carry on a long conversation. With little to do but wait, Ben fell asleep.

Ben woke when the dragon snorted. It raised its head and its tail thrashed back and forth. It very slowly pushed itself up, beginning with its shorter front legs. The dragon unfolded each wing, one at a time, and stretched it. Then it turned and walked towards the cage, its tail dragging behind it.

The dragon appeared old. Its skin was wrinkled and the wisps of hair on top of its head were gray. It was a mustard green color on its underside and a faded grass green on the upper body. Its scales were dull and faded. Sharp claws tipped the end of each of its five-toed feet. Sharp teeth protruded from both the bottom and top jaw. Along the spine was a series of bony ridges. As it drew closer Ben saw that it had brilliant green eyes.

Ben knew the dragon could speak, but he was not prepared for the words spoken in a deep gravelly voice. "Ah, we have new dinner guests."

The dragon laughed as if at some secret joke. It jumped forward and landed near the cage. "You and you," the dragon said, as it beckoned to Ben and Jared. "Come here."

Ben and Jared stepped back away from the dragon.

"Don't make me come and get you," the dragon said. "Otherwise I might decide that both of you look good for supper tonight."

Gill pushed Jared forward towards the fence. Ben followed behind Jared, although everything within him wanted to get as far away as the cage allowed. The two boys stood side by side. Their knees felt weak, and their hands shook as the dragon looked down on them.

"What do we have here?" the dragon said. Neither Ben nor Jared replied, but the dragon did not seem to expect a response. The dragon first turned his attention to Jared. "I think we have a would-be rescuer here. Came to rescue your brother, did you? Impossible, but very brave. I should reward such bravery. If you like, I will eat you first so you do not have to watch your brother die."

The dragon then turned to Ben, "Now who is this with you? You are not one of those pesky heroes are you? I've eaten one or two heroes in my day. Are you from this world or another? Don't answer that," The dragon commanded. "I like to solve mysteries on my own."

Ben swallowed and nodded his head.

"Come closer," the dragon said.

Ben stepped closer.

"Green eyes!" the dragon continued. "You're not a relative of mine are you? Of course not! I know all my pesky relatives. But what are you?" the dragon demanded even more insistently.

Ben remained silent, unsure of what to say.

"Come closer," the dragon demanded again.

Ben stepped closer. The dragon reached through the cage with one of his front legs and dragged him closer still. The dragon's breath was hot on Ben's face. "Time for a taste test," the dragon said. The dragon's tongue whipped through the fence and across Ben's cheek.

"Hmmm, you do not taste like a Lushakan human. You do not taste like a mer. You must be a Chosen of the guardian, but from what planet? I've never tasted anything quite like you on any of the six worlds. Yet there is something vaguely familiar, something that I can't put a name to. Let's see what gifts you were given."

The dragon sat back on his hind legs and tail. It took off a medallion that hung around his neck. Ben gasped. The dragon had the same medallion as Miss Templeton and Lea Waterborn.

"Morton," the dragon commanded, "Come here."

Morton did as he was directed. He came over to where the dragon and Ben stood. Jared stepped out of the way, hoping that the dragon had lost interest in him. The dragon slipped the medallion over Morton's neck, but held tight to both the medallion and Morton.

"Use the medallion," the dragon demanded. "Let us find out what gifts, if any, this boy has."

Morton took the medallion and held it over Ben's hand. As he did so, Ben felt his hands and feet develop suction cups. He then disappeared and became invisible. The dragon held Ben with one clawed hand, and Morton with the other. Morton held the medallion over Ben's hand for several minutes waiting for the revelation of the third gift. When it did not reveal itself, Morton dropped the medallion and let his hand fall to his side. The dragon took the medallion away from Morton and let go of him. The old man fell to the ground.

"A hero, with only two gifts, who tastes strange. What can it mean? Why were you sent with just two gifts? What world are you from? Morton, my friend, can you think of any reason why this boy would be sent out with just two gifts? Any idea who or what he is?"

Morton shook his head. He kept his eyes down so the dragon did not see the hope that had been born in them.

"The Guardian must be losing it," stated the dragon. "For there is no way this boy is any sort of threat to me. Not even fifty more like him would be a threat. I expected better from the high and mighty Guardian." The dragon's voice was full of distain. "Tell me, hero, where are you from?"

"Earth," Ben whispered.

"You lie. I know what an earthling tastes like and you are not it. Why were you given only two gifts?"

"I don't know and neither do the Watchers."

"You are young to be chosen. Is this your first time?"

Ben croaked out a quiet, "Yes."

The dragon sat back on its haunches and laughed. "Well, Morton, if you ever hear from the Guardian again, give my thanks for sending some entertainment. When he no longer amuses me I think I'll feed him to my birds. I don't really like the taste of him myself, but the tregs will eat anything."

The dragon yelled at the ape-man who stood on the platform watching. "Brownie, order one of the tregs to bring some chain!"

The small man turned to his monitors and touched the keypad in front of him. Soon one of the tregs rose from where it sat and flew over the cage to the other side of the metal box. It picked up a chain and carried it to the cage where the bird dropped it at the dragon's feet.

"Morton, my friend," the dragon said, "come here."

The old man shuffled over without raising his eyes to look at the dragon. He stood beside Ben with his hands clenched tight.

"Do I have to tell you everything?" the Dragon roared, "Pick up the chain and bind this creature to the cage. We will keep him standing in this spot tonight. Perhaps he has a third gift. I wouldn't want him to turn into rubber and bounce out of here. Not that he poses any real danger to me, but I'm too old to play the kind of games a would be hero likes to play."

The dragon pulled Ben, now visible, tightly against the fence. Morton picked up the chain and without looking at Ben or the dragon threaded it through the fence and wrapped it around Ben. Morton snapped the padlock shut and dropped the key in his pocket.

"That," the dragon said, "will give me some time to work out the mystery of what world you are from. By the way, you taste bad. I won't bother keeping you as emergency rations. I'll keep you alive until I discover what you are and where you come from. After that I'll kill you and my birds can have you for breakfast."

Ben shuddered. The dragon laughed. "This is so much fun. Thanks for dropping in."

The dragon turned to walk away, "I will be back later to decide who to have for supper," he said. "Will it be Lushakan human? They really are the best tasting. But no, perhaps this is the night for mer? Yes, perhaps mer. It's not good to be picky and let perfectly good food spoil."

The dragon took a few more steps and then turned back.

"Good try, Morton, but I will have that key," the dragon said.

The dragon took the key to the instrument panel and hung it on a hook. He then spoke to the occupant of the metal box. Ben heard a sharp, defiant female voice speaking through the bars of the window. The dragon laughed and then moved on to speak to the ape-man who watched the monitors.

"Who's in the box?" Ben asked the old man.

"A dragon," Morton replied.

"The box is too small to hold a dragon."

"She came as a dragon, but transformed into a woman. Zork...

"Zork?" Ben interrupted.

"The old dragon became a man and they sat down to eat and drink. He gave her a goblet. Zanderella drank. That was a mistake. Zork gave her something to keep her from transforming. He transformed into a dragon himself, picked her up and put her in the box where she has been locked up ever since. Zanderella cannot transform as long as she is in that box. She has been there for over a month now."

"How do you know these things?"

"I saw her arrive. She trusted the old dragon. He tricked her. She called out to him for the longest time, calling him uncle. The dragon just moved further away so that he could sleep without being disturbed. Sometimes at night she cries and it is enough to break the heart of anyone but that dragon."

The man turned and started to walk away.

"Wait!" Ben said. "How long have you been here?"

"Too long."

"How many people have you seen the dragon eat?"

"Too many."

"How did you get here?"

The old man looked from Ben over to the dragon. "Enough with your questions," Morton said and walked away to sit by himself.

The three Lushakan humans came over to where Ben was chained to the fence.

"So it's true," Gill said. "You're from another world. You should have become invisible and stayed invisible when that bird dropped you into the cage."

"It seemed rather cowardly when the rest of you had no choice. Besides," Ben said, "there is a limit to the amount of time I can stay invisible."

"If I'd known you had those two gifts, I would have told you to turn on the invisibility, climb out of here, get the crown, and run as far and fast as you could. The war needs to be stopped before more of my people die."

"I don't think I could get through the barbed wire at the top of the cage, and if I could I don't think I could survive alone on this island long enough to get back to the sea," Ben said.

Gill grunted, "It would be a long shot...a very long shot...even with your abilities."

"I saw your footprints," Ben said, "at the stream, by the waterfall. You entered the water, but never left."

"We were picked up by tregs," Gill replied.

"I guessed that," said Ben.

Ben heard the sound of rummaging. The dragon was walking around the pile of goods. Zork picked up a number of items, examined them and dropped them back down. Ben guessed that the dragon was looking at the things the tregs had picked up during the day when the dragon was asleep. After Zork examined everything of interest, he walked towards the cage. The occupants, except for Ben, moved as far away from the dragon as they could get.

"Oh no," Arno said. "It'll likely be you or me, Gill."

"It's going to be O.K." Gill said. "There are still five tregs to come in. They will bring food for the dragon."

"I'm coming to get you," said the dragon, laughing. "Time to barbecue."

Fire erupted from the dragon's nostrils, aimed at the occupants of the cage. Ben felt the fire's heat on his right side as flame shot through the wire towards the three Lushakan humans who were standing in a group. Brina sat off by himself and Morton stood with his back to everyone on the far side of the cage.

The dragon spread his wings and made a flying jump to the cage and landed close to where the three Lushakans stood. The occupants of the cage ran across to the other side.

"Oh, don't play hard to get," said the dragon. "I really don't feel like eating any of you for supper tonight. Let's have a story while we wait to see if my birds bring something delicious to eat. If they bring something I like, you might all live to see another day. Now, who has a story for me?"

The occupants of the cage were silent.

"No one has a story? Then we'll skip it and go right to dinner."

Gill stepped forward, "I will tell you a story. Long ago, it is said that the mer and human Lushakans were one people. Both races were equally at home on land and sea."

"Heard it already!" the dragon roared. "You'll have to do better than that! Besides, I'd like to hear from the one who tastes so strange."

Ben's mind went blank. He did not know what to say. Finally he began to tell a Robert Munsch story that his grandmother read him years ago. It was the story of a princess whose castle was destroyed by a dragon. The dragon took the prince the princess was to marry. Ben told of how the princess defeated the dragon by flattery, wearing nothing but a paper bag.

The dragon stared at Ben in puzzlement. "I do not like that story." A puff of smoke came out of the dragon's mouth with each word. "I tire of this game. Ready or not, here I come."

The dragon rose into the air and hovered above the occupants of the cage. They could feel the movement of air as its wings beat above them. They heard his voice saying, "Einie, meenie, miney mo, one of you will have to go."

The occupants of the cage cringed in fear. Then, there was a screech as three tregs came into the valley from a day of hunting. Two of them carried sheep-sized rabbits. Another carried a large fish. The dragon took the fish and ripped it apart. He threw the largest part into the cage where Arno picked it up. Arno handed out portions of the fish to everyone but Brina. No one had enough to satisfy their hunger. Ben looked at the piece he'd been given and wished it was at least twice as much. He never dreamed the day would come when he would gladly eat raw fish.

The ape-man came to stand near the dragon with his head bent. It did not look up. The dragon threw the remains of the fish at his feet. The ape-man did not look at the dragon as he picked up the fish. The brownie took the fish over to the coffin box where he cut the fish in two parts and held the smallest part up to the window in the metal box. Ben saw a hand reach out and take it.

"Make sure you feed the mer this time," the dragon said before he turned away from the cage. "I don't like to have emergency rations go bad before I get a chance to eat them. Mer taste bad enough, let alone when they are nothing but scale and bone."

Arno took the fish out of Ben's hand, tore it in two and reluctantly threw the smallest piece into the merman's lap. Brina took hold of the fish as if he feared it would disappear. He shoved the whole thing in his mouth, lay back and closed his eyes as he chewed and swallowed. Ben realized that this was the first food the merman had seen since being taken captive. Ben tossed his fish into Brina's lap.

Brina opened his eyes and looked at Ben, "You sure?" he said.

Ben replied, "You need it more than I do."

Brina took as big a bite as he was able. He was fearful that Arno or Gill would come and take this food away.

"Thank you!" he said to Ben when the food was gone. "You have my undying gratitude. Of course, that might not last very long."

The dragon had turned its attention to the two animals the tregs had brought. Zork breathed fire, which caught the animals as they ran. They died quickly. The fire burned away the creature's fur and roasted them at the same time. The dragon ate them and afterwards the tregs swooped down to pick the flesh off the bones the dragon discarded.

After he finished eating, the dragon stopped by the cage. "You were all very lucky today," Zork said. "You have one more day to live. Tomorrow, Chosen of the guardian, if I can't figure out which world you come from, I will make you tell me before I feed you to the tregs."

Zork walked slowly back to where he was when Ben first saw him. The dragon sat down on his haunches and lowered his head to the ground. The sun was disappearing behind a mountain as the dragon fell asleep.

CHAPTER NINETEEN

THE DRAGON WAKES

As night wore on Ben could hear Jared and the other two Lushakans' whispered conversation. Eventually they fell asleep and there was silence, except from the center of the valley where the dragon lay. The dragon was muttering in its sleep, its scales rubbing against one another as it moved restlessly in the night. A dark shadow slid up beside Ben. Morton's voice whispered, "You had better hope that Zork does not wake up, for his mind is troubled about you. He does not sleep soundly this night."

"You know much about this dragon," Ben stated.

"We have a long history together. Once we were friends. Now he is the enemy of those who serve the Guardian. The other dragon's name is Zanderella. She is a Chosen. She is also Zork's niece. Zanderella made the mistake of thinking Zork would listen to her, because of the bond of affection that once existed between them. She let him trick her. That was the last time that Zork has been a man. He grows more distant from humankind with every passing day."

"The medallion the dragon has belongs to a Watcher, doesn't it?"

"Yes."

"Which world is it from?"

"The same world the dragon is from. Zargon is in great peril as long as the medallion is missing. No one can leave that world, and the Guardian cannot send anyone to it."

"How did Zork come to have the medallion?"

"He took it from the Zargonian Watcher."

"Why would the dragon want the medallion?"

"He is growing old and is afraid of death. The medallion will prolong his life. With it he might cheat death for many centuries. The Medallion also enables him to hide on this world. This mountain is a blank spot to Lea Waterborn: partly because of the medallion, and partly because Zork brought Zargonian soil to this place long ago. Even then, he knew a day might come when he would need a place to hide."

Ben was silent for a moment and then asked his next question. "Are you the Watcher of Zargon?" There was no response. Morton had drifted off into the night.

The chains held Ben tightly against the fence. He could turn his head, but nothing else. He was tired but too uncomfortable and afraid to sleep. He was desperate to stretch and move. As the night wore on and everyone else was asleep, he heard faint sobs coming from the metal box. His heart went out to its occupant. What would it be like to be locked in a box for weeks? Like the rest of them, the dragon girl was trapped with no way out. However, her box did have a door. If someone was willing, they could release Zanderella from her prison.

The cage he was in had no door. The only way out was up. The only ones capable of flying them out were the dragon or the tregs. And the only person with any chance of climbing out was chained and could not move. Thinking these thoughts, with the heartbreaking sobs in the background, Ben's own eyes filled with tears.

Words flowed out of Ben's mouth. "Guardian of the Six Worlds, if you know of our troubles, send help…please."

Shortly after speaking these words, Ben's eyes closed and his head dropped down towards his chest.

Ben woke up when someone shook his arm. The first morning light was just beginning to penetrate the darkness when Ben opened his eyes.

"Ben, wake up," a voice whispered.

"Charla!" Ben's voice was loud in the quiet of the night. Charla and Ben stood silent, both afraid that his voice had awoken someone or, worse yet, something. Indeed it had. On a mat near the treg control center, eyes opened in a furry face. Ben spoke again, more quietly this time. "Charla, how did you get here?"

"I followed the stream up. It goes underground for quite a ways. You could not have come that way. Neither could Jared. Only one who is Waterborn can travel that way, or those Chosen with the gift of breathing under water. The stream takes many routes. I followed many dead ends as I looked for a place large enough to pass through. I finally found a place where it was possible to squeeze through, but anyone bigger would not have made it. So I am here to rescue you once more, but I can't find the door to this cage. Where is it?" Charla spoke so quietly that Ben could hardly hear her.

"There is no door."

"There must be. How would you get in otherwise?"

"Tregs and dragons don't need a door."

"There's a dragon!" Charla said much too loudly.

"Shhh!" Ben whispered. "There is."

Charla fell silent as she digested this bit of news.

Meanwhile the creature near the treg control panel murmured to itself. "What brownie do? They hate dragon. I hate dragon. Maybe they help Zanderella? I want help Zanderella, but don't want dragon to hurt me. Maybe dragon kill all of them and me too. What to do? What to do?"

"The dragon," Ben continued, "says he's going to kill me. He knows that I'm a Chosen. The people here are his emergency rations. One of the prisoners has seen him eat Lushakans: both human and mer."

"That can't be."

"It's true," Ben said, his voice once more too loud. "The best thing you can do is grab the crown and get out of here as fast as you can. Go back to Lea Waterborn. Tell her of the situation and perhaps she can do something."

"I don't understand. Lea Waterborn should know there is a dragon. This is her world. She's the Watcher of Lushaka. This just shouldn't be."

"She doesn't know because the dragon has stolen a Medallion from the Watcher of Zargon. He has also scattered Zargonian soil in this valley. This mountain does not exist to Lea Waterborn."

Charla was stunned, silenced by what she had heard. Then she said, "What of Jared? Is he here with you?"

"Yes," Ben replied.

"And Brina?"

"Yes." Ben was struck by the fact that it was Jared who Charla asked for first.

"There is no way I am leaving any of you here. Getting off this island would take at least a day, if I made it at all. By the time I got to Fairwaters and came back with help, anything could happen."

"Charla," Ben said urgently, "You cannot take on a dragon and a couple of dozen tregs all on your own. The best thing you can do is take the crown and go. And if there is a choice between your life and the crown, go without it. That is the only thing you can do for us. You must save yourself. Jared and Brina would tell you the same thing. You will give us hope by taking word to Lea Waterborn."

Charla and Ben jumped when a voice whispered near them.

"Boy, you just asked the Guardian to send someone to help you and when the Guardian does you want to send her away?" Morton poked Ben and then spoke to Charla, "There is something you can do mer girl. There is a metal box over there. Our only hope is in that box. Open the door and let Zanderella out. And then you get out of here as fast as you can. Do as the boy says. Take the crown and get word to

Lea Waterborn. Go without the crown if you need to, but stay alive and go."

Ben looked toward the box. It stood as a dark shadow in the night. He doubted that letting the dragon girl out would make their situation any worse. "Morton may be right. Do it Charla. Open the door. Then get out of here as fast as you can. If you end up in this cage there is no hope for any of us."

Charla moved off into the dawning light towards the metal box. The small furry creature, moved to the control panel. He saw that all but one of the tregs was asleep. All he had to do was push a button and they would all be awake. They would see the girl and put her in the cage with her friends. Brownie put his finger over the button.

Ben looked up to the cliff tops anxiously. One of the tregs was awake. It was staring down into the valley, but not at the cage. Its attention was on the center of the valley where the dragon lay sleeping.

Ben turned his attention to what the treg was looking at and his heart sank. He could hear muttering. It was not the intermittent muttering that was part of a troubled sleep, but it was the sound of someone talking to themselves. The pile of assorted goods was being shifted. Then the dragon let out a great roar.

"Here it is. This is from Earth. The Guardian's Chosen is from earth! Why does he not taste like an earthling?"

The rustling sound of dragon scales could be heard coming closer. Then came the sound of wings moving air. The dragon landed in front of Ben on the inside of the cage. Zork was holding Ben's gym bag.

"Who are you?" the dragon roared. "Who is your father? Answer quickly or I will start by cooking your feet and move upwards. You will answer me for the pleasure of a quick death."

Ben decided that nothing was to be gained by refusing to answer. "Andrew Taylor," Ben whispered.

"Who?" The dragon roared. The occupants of the cage and the girl in the metal box woke up. The sleeping tregs also woke up, stretched their wings and rose into the air. They wove in and around each other shrieking loudly, unsure of what was expected of them. The air vibrated with their shrieks.

Brownie moved his finger off the button. There was no need to bring the birds now. The brownie moved closer to Charla and the metal box. Charla looked up at the sound of his footsteps and their eyes met. Above them, a treg screeched. Charla reached over her shoulder and pulled out her spear. She stood with the spear held in front of her, her back against the metal box. The first bird came at her from the side. She lunged forward and slashed the bird across its right leg. The treg's cry of pain pierced the air as it veered left. A second and a third bird dove towards Charla. She stood ready to lunge at whichever one reached her first.

The brownie looked at Charla with admiration in his eyes as she stood ready to defend herself against the tregs. Then it moved back to the control panel and pushed buttons. Two birds stopped their dive in mid-air and began to climb. Soon there was not a treg in sight as they all flew away to begin the daily search for food and treasure the brownie sent them on.

CHAPTER TWENTY

FREEDOM

Charla braced herself and pushed upwards on the metal bar that kept the door locked. The bar did not move. Charla threw her full strength into lifting it. It shifted a little and then fell back into place. The bar was heavy, but Charla was also very tired from maintaining her human form.

Meanwhile the dragon continued to roar, "What did you say? Who is your father?"

Ben spoke louder, "Andrew Taylor."

"I know that name," the dragon began quietly, but every word spoken grew louder. "He has been in my brother's house." Suspicion began to grow in the dragon's mind. "Who is your mother?" he demanded quietly, each word spoken distinctly. A puff of smoke escaped from the dragon's mouth with every word.

Ben spoke the only name he knew, "Zinder, Zinder Taylor."

The dragon dropped the gym bag and roared in rage. Flames singed Ben's eyebrows.

"Zinder! You fool! What were you thinking? What is your name, nephew?"

Ben was shocked by the question, but gave his name, "Ben."

"I am sorry to tell you nephew, pardon me great nephew..."

"I am not your nephew!" Ben shouted.

The dragon ignored him and continued speaking, "Your short, but promising life as one of the Chosen of the Guardian is over. I'm tempted to let you live. You would be a nasty surprise for my dear pain-in-the-ass brother. If I could, I would send your dead body to him with a note explaining what his precious daughter has done. He would not be pleased to know that he has a half-breed grandson."

The dragon took a step back and breathed deeply. Ben closed his eyes and hoped death would be quick.

Meanwhile, Charla suddenly found the metal bar easier to lift. A pair of hairy hands had joined hers in pushing it up. Together the ape-man and Charla removed the bar from the door. As soon as the bar was lifted, the brownie ran, and hid trembling behind the control panel. There was the sound of a body hitting the door and Charla found herself on the ground, under a young woman whose greasy hair and unwashed body smelled unpleasant. The young woman's brilliant green eyes were tired and bloodshot. Her face was pale and it was clear that she had suffered from being locked up inside a box.

"Thank you for saving my life," the woman whispered before rolling off Charla and onto the ground. Then she spoke with urgency. "Move, move, get out of my way, right now."

Charla pushed herself up, stood and backed up without taking her eyes off Zanderella. As Charla watched, the freed captive began to change. Blue green scales appeared on her arms and legs and around her neck and face. Her neck began to stretch as did her legs. A tail grew. Wings sprouted from the side of her body.

Zork was focused on Ben, with his back to the metal box. "Goodbye nephew," Zork said, right before Brownie, who had come out from behind the control panel shouted, "Master, master, trouble...She is free."

Zork whipped around to stare at the open door of the metal box. Charla was hidden behind the metal box. Zork did not see her.

"Brownie, what have you done?" Zork roared. "You will regret this." Flames shot out of Zork's mouth as the old dragon took to the air and hurtled towards Zanderella, who had not gone far from the metal box. The female dragon stood with her head hung down beside the box that had held her captive for so long.

"Get back into the box, Zanderella!" Zork roared. "Return to your human form now!"

The young female dragon had no intention of willingly going back inside the box that had held her captive for so long. She took a few faltering steps away from the box towards the center of the valley clearly trying to gain time before she had to face the older dragon.

"I am warning you. Resume your human form and get back in the box or you are dead."

Zanderella did not answer, but continued to stumble slowly away from the box.

"Brownie," the dragon roared as it flew towards Zanderella, "you get those tregs back here now."

Brownie moved quickly in front of the control panel. Charla followed him. Each screen saw the world from the vantage point of one of the tregs. Most were flying over the water, but some were still over the island. Brownie reached out his hand and pushed a button under one of the screens as Charla watched. The image rotated. The bird was retracing its flight back to the volcanic core of the island. Water was soon replaced by a sandy beach and then forest. When Brownie went to push another button, Charla took hold of his hand, and when he looked at her; she shook her head, no.

The brownie stood uncertain as to what to do. He looked at Charla and out to where Zanderella was taking short hopping flights away from Zork.

Charla spoke quietly into the brownie's ear. "I have a friend in the cage, chained to the bars. If we can set him free, he will help us. He has the powers of a Chosen."

Brownie shook his head firmly and pulled his hands free of Charla. Ben's powers were no match for Zork's. Charla moved between him and the control panel. Brownie was strong. He easily pushed Charla aside and stood with his finger over the button. All he had to do was push it and another Treg would return to the valley. He stood with his finger poised. Tears welled up in his eyes. He stood with his finger on the button but he could not push it. Instead he took the key from where it hung on the hook and gave it to Charla, with a nod of his head towards Ben. Brownie sat down on the floor beside the control panel. His whole body trembled. He closed his eyes and put his hands over his ears.

Charla ran across to Ben and put the key in the padlock. The chains fell away.

Zanderella flew up to perch up on a rocky outcropping. Her head hung down. Her sides heaved from the effort of flight. Fortunately, Zork was moving slowly. He was not in the best of health. He was no longer young and had little exercise over the past few months. As Zork rose slowly into the air, Zanderella propelled herself off the cliff towards him. Zork tried to dodge, but he was too slow. Zanderella hit Zork from above and drove him into the ground. They struggled on the valley floor, as cats do, attacking one another with teeth and claw. Finally, Zanderella broke free. In her hand was the Watcher's Medallion. She flew towards the cage. Zork roared in anger when he saw Zanderella with the Medallion. Fire shot out of his nostrils and encircled Zanderella.

CHAPTER TWENTY-ONE

BEN GETS HIS WINGS

Ben called forth his suction cups and was about to climb the wire fence. He wasn't sure what he could do, but he was determined to do something.

"Wait," said Morton, "you're making a mistake." The occupants of the cage looked at Morton. "You," Morton said, pointing at Ben, "are of the Dragon kind. You must transform and fight as a dragon. Only one who is dragonborn has a chance to defeat Zork."

"No, I'm not…I can't …I"

"You can transform," Morton responded. "I am, or at least I was, the Watcher of Zargon. I can sense these things. You may be only part Zargonian, but you have the ability to transform. The Guardian would not have sent you otherwise. You were the best choice on five worlds. You must be able to transform."

Everyone's eyes were focused on Ben. Hope was alive in their eyes for the first time. Ben closed his eyes and thought of himself as a dragon.

Morton commanded, "Stand back everyone, this boy is going to need more room."

Ben thought of himself as a dragon, but when he opened his eyes nothing had changed. Disappointment was clearly visible in the eyes of those around him. Only Morton still had a look of expectant hope in his eyes.

Ben glanced over to the two dragons battling outside the cage. Zork was holding Zanderella down on the ground. Zanderella had put the Medallion over her head and he was trying to get it back. Every time he came close her jaw snapped shut. Zork had her upper body pinned down, but Zanderella's back legs were clawing at him. Zork's claws raked at Zanderella's face and neck. Zork was winning the battle. Ben doubted that the young dragon could hold on for very long, weakened as she was from weeks in the metal box.

Ben wished with every fiber of his being that he could become a dragon so he could help Zanderella. And with that he felt himself changing. His hands were scaly and tipped with claws. He looked behind himself and saw a dragon body complete with tail. His body was green, but had a bluish sheen. Wings grew out of his side. The wing tips were blue.

Ben launched himself into the air. He hit the side of the cage and crashed down. He was still on the inside of the cage. Flight was not as easy as it looked when Zork and Zanderella did it. Neither was it easy to pick himself up off the ground. The wings got in his way until he figured out how to fold them.

Ben stood up and launched himself into the air again with his muscular hind legs. This time he crashed down on the outside of the fence. He untangled his legs and wings and pushed himself up from the ground. He took a few steps and tripped on his own wings. He stood up again and held his wings higher. With wings beating, Ben took short, hopping flights toward Zork and Zanderella. His movement was erratic. Twice he tripped himself up and fell face forward on the ground. Sometimes his feet were on the ground. At other times they were not, as his wings took him aloft. As he came close to Zork and Zanderella, he stopped beating his wings and concentrated on moving his legs in a coordinated manner. Ben crashed into Zork and knocked him off Zanderella with such force that Zork tumbled head-over-heels.

The older dragon pushed himself up and roared in rage. Fire exploded from his nostrils and surrounded Ben. Ben closed his eyes and stepped back. The fire burned, but did not damage his scales. It felt like nothing more than a bad sunburn. The older dragon launched himself into the air and landed on Ben. Ben was not coordinated but he was strong. It was not difficult for Ben to throw the older dragon off. Ben stood up, tripped on his right wing and fell on top of Zork. It was not a planned strategy, but it worked. Ben's weight kept the older dragon down on the ground.

Zanderella stood above them. Green eyes glinted from her freshly scarred dragon face. "Zork, it is time for you to give up."

"Never!" Zork roared. "Brownie, where are those tregs?"

Brownie stood up on shaking legs and turned towards the control panel. Above them the solitary treg he had called screeched. Brownie saw what the treg saw, and the treg had its eyes on Charla.

Zanderella flew over to Zork's pile of treasures. She tossed things this way and that. A gold crown inlaid with pearls went flying into the air. Charla ran to pick it up. As she did so the treg dove towards her. The brownie stood shaking in front of the monitor watching the treg dive towards Charla. He pushed a button and the giant bird banked left and flew out of the valley towards the ocean. Charla picked up the crown without knowing how close she had been to ending up in the cage with Brina and Jared.

Zanderella found the bottle she was looking for. Meanwhile the older dragon was doing his best to break free, arching his back and thrashing his tail, roaring and slashing at Ben with teeth and claws, but Ben could not be budged. Zanderella threw the contents of the bottle into Zork's open mouth. Zanderella grabbed Ben's arm and yanked, "Get off him quickly!"

Ben rolled off the old dragon and watched as Zork shriveled up to become an aged man with thinning silver gray hair and a crease-lined face. Zanderella picked Zork up and carried him to the metal box. She placed him inside the box and closed the door, locking it with the metal bar. She flew into the cage, picked up Morton, and dropped him on the ground outside the cage. Brownie grabbed hold of Morton's legs, and stood attached to him like a young child who has just found a lost parent. Morton gently stroked Brownie's head. Zanderella gave Morton the Medallion. As soon as the old man had the Medallion in his hands, he disappeared out of sight taking Brownie with him.

Another short flight brought Zanderella over to where Ben stood beside Charla. "Thank you," she said.

Charla was still staring at the spot where Morton had disappeared. "Where did he go?" she asked.

"Back to Zargon. The Medallion gives many powers to the one rightfully entrusted with it. My uncle hoped to learn to control it, but never did." Zanderella then turned to Ben. "Who are you?"

"Ben Taylor."

"I don't know that name. I thought I knew every dragon-bearing family on Zargon. Why didn't you transform right away?"

"I didn't know I could."

"This is a mystery I wish I had time to solve. My uncle is not the only one who likes to solve mysteries. But I must go before the portal Morton opened closes. I must take my uncle back to Zargon while I am able."

Zanderella flew to the metal box and perched on top of it.

"Before you leave," Zanderella said, "destroy this thing Zork built to control the tregs. You do not want it falling into the wrong hands. Try to be gone three hours before sunset, as the tregs start to return then."

"Wait!" Charla yelled, as Zanderella rose up into the air. "How are we going to get out of this valley?"

"You have a dragon."

"Yes, but, he can't fly!"

"Every dragon can fly."

"Wait!" Ben said. "I really can't fly."

"Then you'd better learn quickly," said Zanderella. "Come visit me, Ben Taylor. Morton can tell you where to find me. I live with my father Zane and my sister Zinder."

Before Ben could respond Zanderella disappeared, taking the metal box with her. Ben stood in shock, the name Zinder resonating in his ears. He had just met his mother's sister and his grandfather's brother.

CHAPTER TWENTY-TWO

A NEW STUDENT

The sun was high overhead before Ben mastered flight. He was battered from hitting the cliff walls and the valley floor. Perched on the highest point of the island, Ben looked down into the valley. Charla sat leaning on the cage on the outside between Brina and Jared who were leaning against the cage on the inside. The three of them were deep in conversation. Gill and Arno were off by themselves, but close enough to overhear what the other three said. Charla held the Mer King's crown in her lap. It took a moment for Ben to realize what it was she held. He had forgotten the crown and its importance with all that had happened since dawn.

Ben leapt off the cliff and glided down to land rather awkwardly inside the cage close to Brina and Jared. His voice, when he spoke, did not sound like his own. It was deeper and somewhat scratchy.

"I think I'm ready." Ben said. "I will take Brina and Charla to the sea, and retrieve one of the boats before coming back for the rest of you. Jared will be able to take Gill and Arno home."

"Jared's not going home," Charla announced.

"Brina and Charla think Lea Waterborn might welcome a human student at her school," Jared said with excitement. Gill and Arno drew closer.

"Brina and I are agreed," Charla said. "Jared belongs at Fairwaters."

"Ben, you can carry Jared to the school on your back," Brina said, his voice still weak. "The Watcher will want him to be blindfolded so that he does not know the way to the school if he is not accepted."

"Why?" Charla asked. "Lea Waterborn can erase his memory. He doesn't need a blindfold."

"I don't mind wearing a blindfold," Jared said soothingly.

"He will be accepted," Charla said firmly. "And I still don't think a blindfold is necessary."

Jared's brother was listening intently, "Why would he not be accepted. Jared is as capable and brave as anyone you can name. Your school would be lucky to have him. You will know what a real hero is like with Jared there."

"He is a good choice in my book," Ben said softly. Then he said more loudly, "Who wants to be the guinea pig so we can see if I am able to carry someone and fly?"

"Guinea pig?" Gill said, clearly not understanding.

"I think it has something to do with being first," said Jared as he stepped forward.

Ben knelt down and Jared stepped on his front leg and hoisted himself over Ben's neck to sit just in front of his wings. Ben was surprised at how light Jared was. Ben hardly noticed there was someone on his back as he leapt into the air. Soon all the prisoners were on the outside of the cage.

"Are you ready?" Ben asked Charla and Brina.

Charla looked down at the crown she held in her hands. Then she walked over to Gill and placed the crown in Gill's hand.

"It would be best if the Mer King receives this back from your people," Charla said.

A look of surprise, but also of great pleasure was clearly written on Gill's face. He smiled at Charla.

"Thank you changeling. You have a friend among my people— someone besides my brother, that is, for he is your truest friend. Should you ever have need, call, and I will answer."

Ben knelt so that Charla could climb up. The tired mermaid could not make it up on her own, so Jared stepped up and gave her a boost. Ben picked Brina up in his front claws and rose into the air. The humans watched as Ben disappeared from their sight with the mer Lushakans.

It did not take long to reach the ocean. Ben flew low over the water. Charla dove from his back into the waves. Ben skimmed the water and gently released Brina. He watched with concern as the mer disappeared beneath the waves like a sack of potatoes. Ben circled around overhead until he saw two mer tails break the surface of the water. Charla raised her head and shouted up at him, "See you at Fairwaters. Fly south until you see twin islands then turn east. The next island you see is the one you want."

"I'll be there waiting for you." Ben shouted back.

"I wouldn't count on that," Charla replied, the last of her words fading as Ben flew towards the stream where the boats were anchored. He picked up the smallest of the two boats. It was not easy flying with a boat, but Ben did not have far to go. Ben gently dropped the boat into the waves. Soon Gill and Arno were sailing for home, taking the Mer King's crown with them.

Ben was flying over the forest towards the heart of the island to pick up Jared when he saw a treg returning to the valley. A loud challenging cry tore through the air. Ben wondered what new threat had arrived until he realized that the voice was his own. He was shocked by the sound. It was similar to the sound he had often heard in his dreams.

Two tregs were in the valley when Ben reached it. They had Jared cornered. He was keeping the tregs at bay with his spear. Ben landed nearby, unsure of what to do; however, instinct took over and fire erupted from within. The fire surrounded the closest bird. The other treg made a quick escape and rose to sit on a ledge at the far end of the valley.

"Are you hurt?" Ben asked. Jared's shirt was torn and covered with blood.

"Just a scratch," replied Jared, his voice shaky.

"Wait here," Ben said, "while I destroy the control panel."

Ben tore the roof off the control panel. It flew through the air, hit the ground and broke into pieces. Ben was surprised at how very strong he was. He took a deep breath and flame melted the monitors and control panel. Soon there was nothing left that could be used to control the tregs.

Ben picked up his gym bag and a piece of cloth that could be used as a blindfold. Then he stopped long enough for Jared to climb on his back before flying out of the valley. He flew overhead for a moment and watched as the remaining treg dropped down beside the dying one. Ben felt a brief moment of pity for the living bird at the loss of its brother, until he saw it tear the eye out of the dying treg and swallow it.

The trip to Fairwaters did not take long by dragon wing. The sun was sinking from the sky when Ben sighted the island. He dropped down in front of the cave that led into the school. Jared slipped off, still blindfolded. The illusionary snake appeared.

"What's that? It sounds like a snake?" Jared spoke fearfully. He raised his hand to rip the blindfold off.

"Leave the blindfold on until we're inside. Trust me. This snake is just an illusion."

"Wow, it sure sounds like the real thing. Does it look as real as it sounds?"

"I thought so when I first saw it, but now that I've seen the real thing, it's not quite so impressive, though it would still send me running if I hadn't been this way before. Well maybe not," Ben thought, "a dragon can probably take on a snake and win the battle with ease."

Ben transformed into his human form. As a dragon, he was too big to walk into the cave and go through the corridors. He took Jared by the arm and guided him until they stood in front of the carvings on the back wall.

Ben traced one of the carvings. The door did not open. He tried another. It still did not open. He tried several more. Jared stood by his side anxious to take the blindfold off. Ben had only just begun to trace another carved image when the wall began to move.

"Oh, for crying out loud!" a voice said. "A person could wait forever for you to get it right, Ben Taylor."

Charla came out of the cave and put her arm around a blindfolded Jared to lead him forward. Ben followed them in with a look of surprise on his face. As soon as the door closed Charla tore the blindfold off Jared and gave him a hug. Jared winced and it was then that Charla noticed the ripped and bloodied shirt.

"Jared…" Charla began, clearly alarmed.

"It's nothing. Just a scratch," Jared assured her.

"I am taking you straight to the healer. Then it will be nothing. Now it is something." Charla said.

Charla took Jared's hand to lead him down the corridor. Over her shoulder she talked to Ben, "What took you so long?"

"How…?" Ben began.

"I took a shortcut."

"If there was a shortcut why didn't we take it before?"

"The shortcuts are underwater, and you couldn't hold your breath long enough." This last sentence seemed to have a note of accusation in it, as if it was Ben's fault that he could not breathe underwater.

"Couldn't we take the same shortcut on the surface as below?"

"No, the doors are hidden under the sea."

"Doors?"

"Something like what brought you to Lushaka. It is how off-worlders usually get to where they need to go. It's faster and safer too. No tregs. Without the doors it would take months to get to the other side of Lushaka. We were lucky the problem was close to the school this time." Then Charla added, "You have the same kind of doors on earth, I'm sure, but yours are likely not underwater."

Charla continued to hold Jared's hand until they reached the cavern where several students were practicing. Just before they stepped through the door, Charla let go of Jared's hand. Ben guessed that Charla was not yet ready to confront the prejudices that would make it a challenge to have a human as a special friend. Just a few days ago she would have been the most vocal mer at the school in expressing her opinion that a human did not belong at Fairwaters. He thought about how far she had come since meeting Jared for the first time. Ben hoped that the students at the school would give Jared a chance, and that Charla would have the courage to be his friend as he faced the prejudice that was sure to come.

"Lea Waterborn is waiting," Charla said. "She wants to hear a report from each one of us. I've told her Jared was coming. Ben could you go to Lea Waterborn and tell her that Jared has been hurt, and that I am taking him to the healer? You remember how to get to the Watcher's office, don't you?"

"Of course," Ben said. In moments he was climbing the steps that led to where the Watcher's office was. He paused at the top of the stairs to watch mer students in their human form practice several of the things he was learning how to do at Fairhaven. Among other things, some were climbing rock walls, others were climbing rope, some were fencing, and others were doing archery.

Charla and Jared arrived at the Watcher's office just minutes after Ben got there.

"The healer wasn't there. His assistant was. The assistant refused to treat a human," Charla said indignantly. "I tried to tell him that Jared was different from other humans."

"And I tried to tell you that I'm not different," Jared said. "I am just the first human you have gotten to know."

"Well if you had kept your mouth shut she might have helped you," Charla said. "Everyone here knows humans are—"

"Are welcome here in my office," Lea Waterborn broke in. "Welcome to Fairwaters, Jared, courageous and faithful friend to human and mer alike. True friends are the best of all the Guardian's gifts. May you find some true friends within these walls!"

Ben relaxed. The Watcher's welcome of Jared assured him that Jared would not be sent away immediately. The Watcher would give him a chance to prove himself.

Charla smiled. She reached over and squeezed Jared's hand.

"Be seated and food will be brought." Lea Waterborn said. At the mention of food Ben realized he was hungry, very hungry. Images of what would satisfy his hunger were disturbing. They included a whole cow, a few fat sheep and a horse, hooves and all. Ben shook his head and replaced the images with hamburgers, pizza, and pecan pie. When the food arrived there were eggs, sea cucumber, sea slugs, seaweed and other things that Ben could not name. Ben sighed, as he pushed the images of his favorite foods out of his mind and picked up some of everything. Ben continued eating long after everyone elsc was satisfied.

"Now that almost everyone's hunger is satisfied, it is time to speak. We will begin with Brina. It is clear that you have been water-starved. Tell mc all that has happened to you since you left here four days ago," Lea Waterborn demanded.

Brina told his story. When Brina finished speaking, Lea Waterborn said, "You did well, Brina. As hard as it is to be away from water in your human form, it is that much harder when you are in your true form."

"When the others were asleep, Morton brought me water."

"It is hard to believe that the Watcher of Zargon was held captive here on my world and by Zork, no less. Well that explains why that area of Lushaka became fuzzy to me. It also explains why I lost contact with the Watcher on Zargon." Lea Waterborn was silent for a moment and then said sadly, "This would have never happened when Morton was in his prime."

Then looking up at Brina the Watcher said, "Brina, you are truly worthy of being a Chosen of the Guardian."

"I did very little but sit in a cage and wait to be rescued or eaten," Brina said.

The Watcher paused and then said, "Charla, it is your turn. I am particularly interested in why you disobeyed me." There was a frown on the Watcher's face.

"I only planned to follow Brina and Ben as far as the Island. I would have come back if Brina hadn't been taken by the tregs."

These words caused Brina to grunt in disbelief.

Charla gave Brina a dirty look and continued with her story. "When Brina was taken away, I was sure that you would want me to do something to save him. I sent Ben to…"

Charla stopped. She knew there was no way to tell her story in a way that would not get her into trouble. The Watcher had said Ben was not to go to the human community and she had sent him there partly because she did not want to be in the company of a human.

"Watcher," she finally said, "you were right, I wasn't ready. I couldn't maintain my human form when I was afraid. I didn't have wisdom when I needed it."

"And," the Watcher added, "you allowed your own prejudices to jeopardize the Guardian's work. Prejudice always interferes in the quest for peace. You were right when you said you were not ready, but you soon will be. To know that you have limits and can fail like everyone else is an important part of being ready. I hope you also learned that prejudice can be costly and interfere with right thinking and acting."

Shame filled Charla; she closed her eyes and bowed her head.

"May I say something on Charla's behalf?" Jared asked.

He was afraid of interrupting the Watcher, but felt that he had words that must be spoken.

Lea Waterborn gave permission with a brief nod.

"Charla did something very noble. She found the crown and had it in her hands. She could have returned with it and got the credit for stopping the war, but she gave the crown to my brother Gill because she thought it would be a help for human Lushakans in negotiating with King Somos. She did this even though my brother did not treat her and Brina with the respect they deserved."

"Very good! Thank you Jared. You have done very well, Charla. I am pleased with your quick thinking and the courage you displayed, but more than that I am pleased that you were able to think of the greater good. You are becoming someone I will be proud to send on the Guardian's missions. Come to my office next week and I will give you the test to see whether the Guardian has need of you in the coming months. Meanwhile, you have three months of detention. I specifically told you not to go. This time it turned out to be the right thing, but I don't want you to think that you can disregard the wisdom and insight I have as a Watcher. Next time you may not be as fortunate to find true friends to journey with."

"But..." Charla began. Then stopped and said, "I will report to the kitchen later."

Brina came to her rescue. "Watcher, I know Charla should not have disobeyed, but we would still be in that cage without her."

"I concede that in this situation good came from the wrong that Charla did. However, I still think it is important for her to learn a lesson. I have been the Watcher a long time. Other students have disobeyed my instructions. Few were as lucky as Charla."

"Brina, I am resigned to doing kitchen duty for three months," Charla said. "It might even teach me something."

Lea Waterborn laughed, "Charla, is it really you, or has an imposter come back to Fairwaters? I will give a little on this. Instead of three months, you will have kitchen duty for six weeks."

Lea Waterborn turned to Jared, "Now Jared, it is your turn."

"I did not do much," Jared said.

"From what I have heard from Charla, you did your part. You showed real courage and helped ensure the peace of our world for now. Not only that, but you helped send a Watcher back to his own world. Who knows what was going on in Zargon with Morton's absence? A world without a Watcher is a world in serious trouble. Two worlds have reason to be grateful to you."

"Still, my part was small," Jared said.

"That's not true," Charla exclaimed passionately. "We would not have made it very far without Jared."

Ben nodded his agreement.

"Jared belongs at Fairwaters," Charla added with passion.

"We will see," replied Lea Waterborn. "Jared, you have won Charla's approval and that has not been an easy thing to do in the past. Perhaps she will be less quick to judge the shortcomings of others in the future.

I believe what Charla tells me—you belong here, but whether this is the right time for a human to be a student at Fairwaters is still to be decided. There is much prejudice. I wish it were not so. It should not be so among the Guardian's chosen. You can stay for now. If you choose to leave because there is no welcome here, I will not think less of you. And even if you do not choose, it may be necessary for me to send you away because your presence is a disruption to the peace of the school. If that should happen, I will regret the need to send you away."

"I understand," Jared said. "The prejudice goes both ways. I never dreamed a mer and especially a mer changeling could be a friend."

"It will work out. I know it will," said Charla firmly.

"If anyone can make it so by sheer strength of will it is you, Charla," Lea Waterborn said laughingly.

"I too will help Jared in whatever way I can," said Brina. Jared and Charla both smiled at him in gratitude.

"Your support will go a long way, Brina, for the other students respect you and will be inclined to follow your lead," Lea Waterborn said.

Lea Waterborn turned her attention to Ben, "Ben, tell me your story."

When Ben finished, Lea Waterborn said, "I suspected there was more to you than first appeared. It even crossed my mind that you might be Dragonborn. Those eyes of yours are common among the dragonborn, but anywhere else they are unique. Ben, normally you would stay for an extra day so that your story could be shared with all our students. It helps build their appreciation of the worlds to which they will be sent. It also gives them confidence that the Guardian can accomplish great things through them when it is their turn to go through the portal. However, Mariah Templeton is anxious for your return. She has been anxious from the very beginning, and with each day her anxiety grows. I can feel her anxiety through the bond that we share as keepers of the Guardian's Medallion. She would sleep better tonight if you were back at Fairhaven. So if you wish, I will send you home without the normal formalities. Besides, it would not hurt our students to hear the story told by Jared with help from Charla and Brina."

Ben stood. He was anxious to get home. "I would like to leave today, but I truly hope the Guardian will send me back to this world one day. I have made some good friends here."

Charla gave Ben a hug and a kiss on the cheek. "Good-bye, my friend. The next time we meet I hope it is on your world and I am there as a chosen of the Guardian."

"I hope we meet again on some world," Ben replied.

Brina stepped forward and shook Ben's hand. "Thank you. All Lushakans are in your debt. You have my gratitude now and always. One day I hope to return the favor. Until then, may the Guardian go with you."

"And may your name and your deeds be praised in the halls of the ancestors." Ben did not know where those words came from and why he said them, but from the look of pleasure on Brina's face he knew they were the right ones.

Jared stepped forward and clasped Ben in a short bear hug. "Take care of yourself. I hope we meet again," he said.

"I hope you are accepted here and we meet again," Ben replied.

"I'm counting on it," said Jared smiling.

CHAPTER TWENTY-THREE

A FAMILY REUNION

Lea Waterborn stepped in front of Ben and led the way to the door that would take him back to earth. When she opened the door there was a stone wall. Ben walked towards the wall with his eyes closed. He hung in the air for a moment and then fell about three feet into water that closed over his head. This time it was not a sea, but a deep, square pool made of concrete. It was not large and a few kicks brought Ben to the side of the pool. He threw his gym bag out and prepared to lever himself out of the water.

"Why is there always water?" Ben grumbled, not expecting a reply.

"To keep you from spraining an ankle or busting a leg, for one thing. Now you know why it is important that you learn to swim, Ben Taylor. The water also makes sure you do not bring any germs or bugs that we do not already have on earth back through the portal with you. This water has special cleansing powers."

Allison Sims was sitting on a chair by the wall.

"What are you doing here?" Ben asked, as he wiped the water out of his eyes.

"Waiting for you. Well, not for you especially. I am watching for anyone who might arrive. Someone is always here watching, and now that you are a chosen you will take your turn."

"You've been to another world?"

"Not yet, but I will go one day…who would guess that your first trip would happen on the very day you were tested, and that you would be sent to a world full of water? I worried about you when I heard what world you went to and that you had not been given the ability to breathe underwater."

The thought that Allison worried about him filled Ben with joy.

"If I hadn't had my gym bag, I would have died in the first ten minutes. But this thing is amazing," Ben said holding out his gym bag. "It held air until Charla found me."

"Charla?" Allison asked.

"A Lushakan mermaid who saved my life more than once."

"I can't wait to hear all about Lushaka and what you did there, but you must go to the Watcher now. You need to change into dry clothes first," Allison instructed, pointing to a wooden change house that had been built onto the side of the castle.

Ben dressed quickly and went down the stairs to Mariah Templeton's office.

Mariah Templeton sat at her desk, a cup of tea in her hand, which dropped onto the desk when she saw Ben. There were two people in the room with Mariah Templeton. Someone was sitting in the leather chair that sat in front of Mariah Templeton's desk, and Andrew Taylor sat on one of the chair's overstuffed arms. His one hand was resting on the shoulder of the person who sat in the chair, while the other hand was holding a cup of tea. Andrew Taylor had his back to the door and did not immediately see his son.

"I wouldn't drink that tea, Dad. It does strange things to a person," Ben said softly.

Andrew Taylor deposited the tea unceremoniously on the desk, leapt from the arm of the chair and enfolded his son in a bear hug. When Ben opened his eyes he noted that the occupant of the leather chair had stood and was standing beside Ben and his father. The woman had shoulder-length red hair. Her eyes were closed. Tears were flowing from beneath her eyelids. The woman's eyes opened and Ben tensed. He knew instinctively who she was. The eyes were a brilliant grass green. They were exactly like his.

Andrew Taylor drew back from his son and reached out his arm to draw his wife to his side.

"Ben," he said, "this is your mother."

Ben did not know what to say or do. This woman might be his mother, but to him she was a stranger.

"Um...er...hello," he said lamely and put out his hand so his mother could shake it. The woman ignored his hand. She stepped past it and wrapped her arms around Ben.

Ben stood there with his arms hanging down for a few seconds and then slowly put his arms around his mother to return the hug. His tears joined hers. Andrew Taylor put his arms around the two of them. It was several minutes before any of them were willing to let go.

Meanwhile, Mariah Templeton poured a fourth cup of tea. Ben sat on the other overstuffed chair arm, beside his mother. Mariah Templeton pushed the tea towards Ben.

"It is not the tea that does strange things, Benjamin," she said. "It is the chair. The tea is perfectly safe. It is just plain, ordinary, old-fashioned tea."

Mariah Templeton paused and took a sip from her cup.

"I have been very worried about you—more worried than I have been in four hundred years. It was against my better judgment to send a boy so young, who was terrified of water, to a world of water, without the gift of being able to breathe underwater."

Ben could see that Mariah Templeton looked more tired than she had when he left five days ago.

"Before you came through the door Andrew and Zinder were about to tell me what they are doing here in my office together." Mariah Templeton stressed the word together. "From what I have just seen and heard, it seems that you are part of their story. We will hear what your parents have to say and then you will tell us all about what happened on Lushaka. Andrew. Zinder. Please proceed."

Andrew and Zinder looked at each other to see who would begin their story.

"Zinder and I met on Mellish, the second world," Ben's dad finally said. "We were both far from home for the first time. We knew the rules about not getting involved romantically with someone from another world, but we were alone together for a long time. We fell in love and pledged ourselves to one another. Shortly after that, we were separated. We did not see one another for the next three years. Ben was born after Zinder returned to Zargon and I did not know I had a son."

Andrew looked at his wife, with moisture in his warm eyes.

"I kept Zenjamin's birth secret from my family and friends," Zinder said. "I went and stayed with an old she-dragon I knew who would keep my secret. It is usual for my people to be born with a line of scales down their back, but Ben had none. I lived with Zeemaron for nearly three years, waiting for signs that Zenjamin would be able to transform. He had the green eyes of a Dragonborn but there were no other signs. No smoke when he got mad. No tiny wings sprouting when he wanted something just out of reach. I knew the Dragonborn would never accept a son of mine by a father from Earth who could not transform. They would have a hard time accepting a child who was not pure dragonborn, let alone one who could not transform. I also knew he would find no acceptance among the humans on Zargon because of his green eyes. Only the Dragonborn have green eyes on Zargon. Zenjamin's life would always be in danger if he stayed on Zargon."

Zinder paused to lift her son's hand to her cheek and hold it there.

"The day came," Zinder continued, "when I realized Zenjamin would be better off with his father. I went to see Morton and told him my secret. Morton agreed that the best place for Zenjamin was with Andrew. Morton allowed me to send a message to Andrew by a

Chosen who was coming to earth. I wrote and told Andrew that a package would arrive in twelve days. He was to arrange to be the one watching the pool near midnight."

"Well, I never heard of such a thing," Mariah Templeton snorted. "Morton should never have kept that a secret from me. And what about you, Andrew Taylor, why have you kept this secret from me?

"The night B...Zenjamin arrived I was watching the pool. I traded a shift so I could be there that night. My shift was just about over when there was a splash. I looked up, but saw nothing. I waited, but no one came out of the water. Then just under the surface I saw something. I went into the water and grabbed hold of the bundle. It was dark and I could not see that well. It wasn't until I lifted the package out of the pool that I realized it was a child. Ben had been floating face down in the water. I heard my replacement on the steps and I raced down the stairs past him with Ben under my arms. I ran to the healer's quarters, but she was not there. I stayed in her office and resuscitated Ben on my own. He was terrified and cold. I took him to a room at the far end of the castle. The next day I planned to come and tell you about Ben, but I just did not know what to say. Ben and I left for my mother's house the next day. I didn't tell mother that Ben came from Zargon—just that he was my son. I think she guessed, but I never confirmed her suspicions."

"So that's why I had those bad dreams," Ben interrupted. "Tell me, does Zargon have two moons?"

"Yes," answered his father.

"In my dream there were always two moons," Ben said.

"Now that you know why you had the dreams, it is very possible that you will not be troubled by them again," Mariah Templeton said.

"I think you might be right. And after surviving Lushaka I'm really not afraid of water anymore."

"Benjamin, it is time for you to tell us what happened on Lushaka," Mariah Templeton said, "but first let me pour some more tea for everyone."

As Ben told his story he saw pride in his dad's eyes. Ben was so glad that he had not returned to earth that first day without trying to help the people of Lushaka.

"You are Dragonborn after all," his mother said. She squeezed Ben's hand, which she had been holding all this time. "Morton said you had defeated Zork, but I could not imagine how you did it."

"Poor Morton," Mariah Templeton sighed. "He was an old man when I was a young girl in training. He has longed to lay down the burden of caring for a world for quite some time."

"Three times a new Watcher was chosen and began training, but each time the struggle for power between the Dragonborn families led to that person's death," Zinder added. "Each clan wants to have the next Watcher come from among them. There are times when I am very ashamed by my people, Zenjamin. I hope you have inherited some of your father's desire to live in peace with all."

"Miss Templeton, I would like to take my son away from the school for a few days, if I may," Andrew Taylor said. "I would also like Zinder to come with us."

"I am supposed to be on Mellish," Zinder said. "I do not know how desperate the situation is there."

"Quiet, please!" Mariah Templeton said. She cupped the Medallion in her hand and closed her eyes.

"Zinder, you can stay with Andrew and Zenjamin for two days," the Watcher said after she opened her eyes, "and then you must be on your way to Mellish."

"We will go to Campbell River and rent a cottage," Andrew said. "Zinder and Ben have a lot of catching up to do."

"Fine," said Mariah Templeton. "I hope you will have more time together in the future. Ben, I will see you at the beginning of next week."

"There is something I wish to say before we go," Zinder said. "Zenjamin must go to Zargon for training. He needs to go as soon as possible. The transformations can be difficult and dangerous without training. Some dragonborn fail to make the transformation from human to dragon and back again. When that happens they become creatures that are neither human nor dragon. When I finish my assignment on Mellish, I will make arrangements for Ben to come and train at our school. He has been lucky so far, but his luck will not continue. It might be best for Ben not to transform until then."

"Yes. I agree. Ben should go to Zargon for training," Mariah Templeton said. Andrew Taylor nodded slightly in agreement.

"One more thing," Mariah Templeton said, as they were leaving. "Please do not discuss Ben's ability to transform with anyone else, not even other Chosen."

When Ben went to his dorm room to pick up some clothes he passed Mr. Tanner. "Glad to see you back, Ben," the teacher said. "Your swim test has been rescheduled for Monday morning right after breakfast. It would be wise to bring a swimsuit that fits this time."

"I will, for sure," Ben said.

***

Monday morning at 9:00 a.m. saw Ben in the pool. Phil Tanner, his parents, and the students from his class watched as Ben slid into the water and swam the length of the pool. Ben had no trouble passing the swim test, which surprised every grade nine student except Allison. Water no longer terrified Ben. Perhaps it was his time on Lushaka, and perhaps it was the knowledge that he could fly, breathe fire, and if necessary, lift the roof off the building that gave Ben the confidence he needed.

Ben's class cheered when he passed the test. Afterwards, Ben and his father watched as Zinder walked towards a brick wall that would take her to another world.

Denzel knew Ben had a secret, and that the secret had something to do with his ability to pass the swim test, but no matter what Denzel tried, he could not pry the secret out of Ben. Ben simply said, "Next year—you will know all about it next year."

Thank you for reading Ben the Dragonborn. I hope you enjoyed this first book in the story of the Six Worlds. The second book is entitled Ben and the Watcher of Zargon (September 2015). If you would like to sign up to be notified when new books come out, you can add your name to an email list found on this series Facebook page.

https://www.facebook.com/Benthedragonborn

If you enjoyed Ben the Dragonborn please consider leaving a review. A few simple sentences are all that is needed to make this author's day.

And finally, remember to always seek the treasure of your own true self.

ABOUT THE AUTHOR

Dianne was once asked what kind of animal she would be, if she could be an animal. The person who asked the question was shocked when Dianne said she'd like to be a dragon. There are times in everyone's life when being able to fly high and breathe fire sound very appealing. However, if you can't be a dragon, or have a dragon as a pet, then the next best thing is to write books with dragons in them and get a dog. Dianne lives in the Pacific Northwest with her husband Doug, his three cats and her beloved dog Thomas, who gets Dianne out walking almost every day, which is the next best thing to flying on dragon wing.

Printed in Germany
by Amazon Distribution
GmbH, Leipzig